D1116043

THE MONEY ROOM

· THE ·

MONEY ROOM

Eloise Jarvis McGraw

Weekly Reader Books
Middletown, Connecticut

Copyright © 1981 by Eloise Jarvis McGraw
All rights reserved. Printed in U.S.A.

Weekly Reader Books Edition published
by arrangement with Atheneum

For my husband, William Corbin McGraw—co-progenitor of this story, collaborator in its green-apple stage, and subsequently live-in expert on high finance and filberts as it ripened into something of my own.

THE MONEY ROOM

CHAPTER I

A gold September sun was rising over the little town of Dover, Oregon. The town itself was still in shadow, but on the slope of Indian Hill to the west the early light touched barns and tilting filbert-nut orchards, and at the town's edge, it flashed on the window of a tiny house from which horrendous screeching sounds were issuing.

Inside, a dumpling-shaped old lady with a mole on her chin was saying, "I'm coming, be *patient!*" as she hobbled in bathrobe and slippers across the kitchen toward a big hooded cage. Loosening the ties, she took the cover off the cage and added, "Good morning, George!"

George was a parrot—chunky and silver-gray except for a scarlet tail. He glared at her, made a few more *awrrrrking* noises, then suddenly uttered a loud, chortling laugh and in a deep baritone more suitable to a large man than to a middle-sized parrot, said, "In the *money* room, Dorrie, where else?"

The old lady with the mole on her chin—whose name was

not Dorrie—smiled fondly at the parrot. "You don't have to yell at me," she told it. "I'm not deaf."

It was a little joke between them. She *was* deaf, to many sounds and most voices. But George's she could hear clearly without her hearing aid. She gave him fresh water and some sunflower seeds, on which he began to breakfast noisily while she looked out the kitchen window, watching the sunlight spread down the slope as she waited for her kettle to boil.

"Money room, Dorrie—*awrrrrrrrrk!"* said George, and repeated his chortling laugh.

The old lady smiled, but absent-mindedly, as if her thoughts had drifted, and her gaze moved ahead of the sun to a certain rusty-red barn and old white house halfway down the hill, drowsing above their sweep of filbert orchard like sleepers with the quilt pulled up to their chins. Sighing, she murmured, "Oh, Scotty, how you did enjoy a laugh!"

George cracked another sunflower seed, shuffled sideways on his perch, and regarded her with an amiable eye. He was accustomed to her calling him sometimes by that other name.

On the hillside, in the old white house she was watching, somebody else was being roused from sleep.

"Scotty—*psssst*. Scotty!"

Pause.

"Hey, *Scotty*. You awake?"

A shorter pause. Then the penetrating, insistent whisper came again, as it would continue to do, Scott Holloway felt mortally sure, until he was an old, old man, unless he answered. But for another moment he lay motionless in the rumpled bedclothes, flat on his back as always with both hands beneath the pillow, eyeing with dislike the blotchy, busy pattern of climbing roses on the wallpaper of this unfamiliar room which now was to be his. He was willing to bet Great-Gramp had never chosen that sappy wallpaper. Mrs. Elmer's idea, probably. Or maybe Great-Gram's, because it did look ancient—in fact part of the pattern had faded right out. As the early sunlight advanced across the wall he could see traces of a sort of trellis the roses must have once climbed on. Good riddance. Now if the rest would just fade away, he told himself, trying not to think of the wonderful Stewart tartan wallpaper in his lost, beloved room on Cherry Street back in Medford.

"*Pssssst*. Scotty. Scotteeeee! Aren't you awake?"

Scotty sighed and kicked the covers off. "I am now. Come on in, Lindy. What d'you want?"

His sister Melinda, clad in bright red pajamas, bright blue slippers, and gold-rimmed glasses, pushed open the door and confronted him. Her brown braids curled up on the ends like live things, one cheek was creased and much pinker than the other—Lindy even *slept* hard—and her whole bright-eyed, freckle-faced, sturdy little person vibrated with surplus energy. "I want you to get *up*," she told him. "So we can start!"

"Start?"

"Start hunting for the Money Room, meatball!"

"Oh, that." Scotty grinned. He had known quite well what she meant, and why she'd begun hissing outside his door so early on their very first morning in this house. But it was fun to tease Lindy because she was usually too absorbed in her own purposes to be aware that she was being teased. She was nine—four years his junior, a whole head shorter, and almost his opposite in temperament, build and habits. But they got on well enough—like a couple of trains, Scotty sometimes thought, running amiably on parallel tracks heading for different destinations. Now and then their tracks even merged for a while in some common enterprise—such as the private language called Dobish they'd spent a whole summer inventing, a few years back. Bits of it still surfaced occasionally in Lindy's conversation, to Scotty's embarrassment. He now felt Dobish to be utterly childish.

Obviously their new joint effort—if Lindy had her way—was to be the Great Money Room Quest.

"So get *up*," she was insisting with an impatient bounce.

"Okay, okay, give me a chance. And say 'sir' when you're talking to a superior."

"I'm talking to the slowest snail in the state of Oregon," Lindy told him. "I'm going to get dressed, and then I'm going to drink some milk, and then I'm going to *start*. And if you don't hurry up I'll find that Money Room before you even find your shoes!"

The door closed with a decisive click. After a thorough-going stretch, and a yawn that momentarily put his jaw out of place, Scotty unfolded his string-bean self from the edge of the bed. ("You'll fill out," his mother had assured him. "Once you stop growing upward so fast. You're just kind of a straight line right now." "*I'm* practically a circle," Lindy brooded. "And *you'll* stretch out," their mother had said patiently. "Quit worrying, both of you.")

The sun, by now, had withdrawn its spotlight from the wallpaper roses and backtracked out the window to flood-light the world outdoors. Scotty, absently finger-combing his

dark thatch—already permanently tousled by three cowlicks—
blinked around him at a room stacked with toppling piles of
his belongings, dumped any old place last night. The sight
made him want to lie right back down again. But there was
a come-hither smell of bacon drifting up from below, and
anyway he was hopelessly awake. Cocking his head to glance
in his mirror, which at the moment lay sideways across a suit-
case, he met his own lackadaisical gaze, saw the same old
face—a long triangle set with two lumps of coal and a nose,
the whole much narrower seen in front-view than in profile—
a face Lindy had once thoughtfully likened to a meatcleaver.
("Oh, thanks a lot. Hatchet-faced, you mean," he'd said.)
He gave it a small sneer in passing, let his dispirited gaze
slide past a collapsing brickpile of books, a slither of clothes
on a chair. Same old possessions, looking like displaced per-
sons in this foreign room. They'd get over it tomorrow.
Meanwhile, here today was, stretching ahead of him in the
too-familiar pattern—a day of Back to Square One, Start
From the Beginning, Do the Whole Thing Over. It made him
tired to think of it—to think of the next six months.

Though there *was* one novelty in the same old set-up:
Great-Gramp's legendary (probably mythical) Money Room.
Lindy's idea might not be all bad.

Unbuttoning his pajama jacket, he walked to the window
and stood a moment, looking out, surprised by how high a
perch he now commanded. It was the first real look he'd had
at the old Scott place, now the new Holloway place (though
he was willing to bet nobody would ever call it that.) They
had arrived after dark last night, he and his mother and Lindy,
having spent half of yesterday in Medford overloading the

station wagon, the other half squeezed three-in-the-front-seat on the road. They'd had barely enough ambition left last night to fall into sketchily made beds.

Now he saw that the old house was taller than he'd realized; his second-story windows at the back looked southeast over a slanting sweep of hillside, with a left-hand glimpse of the old rusty barn and some kind of big shed, straight ahead some fruit trees giving way to a grove of dark firs, and to the extreme right, a view downhill—between the grove and the filbert orchard—to the lane at the bottom of the slope. Across the lane, with its ditch heaped and mounded with blackberry vines, and beyond a few stubble fields, he could see the two or three cottages, set any-which-way in their dusty summer's-end gardens, that formed the outskirts of Dover— pop. 3,043. School was in Dover somewhere; grades one through eight, no junior high of course, just plain seventh grade. His third new school in two years. He yanked his mind away from it.

A screen door banged somewhere below, drawing his glance down. His mother's foreshortened figure appeared on the back step, wrestled briefly with a couple of empty cartons, and disappeared with another bang of the door. Scotty's gaze moved on, around a hummocky back yard enclosed by a rail fence loaded with unpruned rose vines. The grass was burned straw-gold everywhere except underneath a huge cork elm tree, where it was still a deep summer green. There was a narrow brick walk out to the pump house, and a crooked little beaten path running kitty-cornered across the grass to the gate. It was the kind of path a dog makes on its daily errands. Maybe Mr. Elmer had owned a dog when he lived here. If so it must be dead now, like Mr. Elmer, or moved away with Mrs. Elmer to her sister's in Seattle. Scotty wondered if a farm dog would be happy in Mrs. Elmer's sister's house, which he pictured as cramped and tidy. Then he wondered if a town-dog like their own Gretel would be happy on a farm.

The Elmers seemed to have left one animal: a horse—unless that was a wooden image standing hipshot in the little pasture behind the barn. Or unless that was a neighbor's pasture. All Scotty knew of the farm's boundaries was that they enclosed twenty-three acres, an area of which he had only the vaguest notion. He hoped it included the fir grove. It had once included a small tenant house with its own half-acre where the Elmers had lived for years—their home for life, by the terms of Great-Gramp's will. But ten years ago when his mother inherited the place she had sold off the Little House bit, transferring the Elmers into the spacious farmhouse instead. The move must have seemed sensible at the time but it had given her large and unexpected headaches in the three years since his father died when she wanted to move here herself. Of the often-regretted Little House itself he could seen no sign.

Well, exploring came next—after some of that bacon. He turned away and reached for his clothes.

He found his family downstairs in the high-ceilinged old kitchen, surrounded by unpacked possessions and a few orphaned-looking groceries. Lindy was eating cereal at the table in the big bay window, accompanied by the loud seed-cracking of Binkie, her lemon-colored parakeet, in the wicker cage at her elbow. His mother, her dark, cropped hair slightly on end but her compact figure already neatly clad in the plaid skirt and shirt Scotty thought of as her Business Suit, was standing at the stove creating delicious aromas in calm disregard of the clutter of boxes and baskets. She was closely watched by a shiny brown dachshund sitting rigid with attention almost under her feet.

"No," she was saying, "I never hunted for it myself because when I came visiting Gran and Gramp I was always too busy having a great time. And anyway—oh, there you are, Scotty. This is your bacon, but first clear some of those cartons out of here. And find Gretel's basket so I can order her into it. Gretel, *move*, please. Lindy, was there a plate wherever you found that bowl? Oh, on that box, Scott. And there's bread and butter somewhere—there, on the counter beside the birdseed. No eggs yet."

"Anyway what?" Lindy prodded.

"Anyway I don't remember that Money Room story as anything but an old family joke. Somebody would say, 'Why, the fellow's worth more than Gramp Scott's Money Room!' Then everybody would laugh. Only sometimes they sort of sighed, too, seems to me." Janet Scott Holloway—known to her family as "Mur" since Scotty's first stab at saying "Mother" —was silent a moment, an abstracted look in her dark eyes. Then she shrugged and took the skillet to the sink. "I don't really remember. I was just a little kid. Scotty, you'll find a knife in that picnic hamper on the floor there."

"But I mean later," persisted Lindy. "When you were in college in California and used to come up here for Christmas vacations and even for whole *summers* because it was so far back to Washington, D.C. . . ."

"Oh, by that time nobody'd mentioned the Money Room in years. Probably forgotten what it was all about."

"But you could've found out! You could've asked Great-Gramp his own *self!*" Lindy pointed out in exasperated tones. "Believe me, if *I'd* been right here with him, every summer—!"

"It was only a few summers really." Mur poured herself a cup of coffee, leaned back against the counter. "Anyhow, I think I did ask Gramp once which room was the Money Room. He just laughed and said they all were, when you considered the way building costs were shooting up. How right he was. If you tried to build a house like this today—! Oh, but it's good to be here! Isn't it?" She sipped her coffee, gazing around the shabby old room with loving eyes.

"Yeah, fine," said Scotty temperately, sitting down with his breakfast.

"Great!" pronounced Lindy. "But listen, Mur. It couldn't be *just* a joke, could it? Maybe it wasn't even a room in this house. Maybe it was at his business or something."

"He didn't have a business. Not after he moved to the farm." Mur's glance had shifted to Scotty.

"Oh, yeah. Well, d'you s'pose he meant a room with a safe in it? Or maybe a basement room he'd *buried* some money in, or—"

"Lindy, you know exactly as much as I do about that Money Room, because I've told you every last thing I remember—and I'm beginning to wish I'd never brought it up. So please—turn the record over. And eat your breakfast." Mur carried her coffee to the table and slid in beside Scotty. "It's our very last move—the last new school. I promise. I know you can't be wildly enthusiastic yet, but—postpone judgment. I used to love this old place when I was your age . . . Scotty, I *know* you'll like it too. Once you get a chance to look around—"

"Yeah, sure. I've already been looking out the window." Scotty fielded his bread on its leap from the toaster and dropped another slice in. "By the way—is that fir woods on this property?"

"Oh, you bet. It's all ours back there—barn, potato cellar, garden, fruit trees—everything back to the creek—and the whole filbert orchard down to the lane. The only thing I ever sold off was that half-acre the Little House is on."

She sighed automatically. Still regretting, Scott thought, that they couldn't have moved out here three years earlier.

"Then the pasture's ours too," he said. "Did you know there was a horse in it?"

"A horse?" chorused his family.

Lindy flung her spoon into the bowl, scooted around the curve of the built-in window seat that encircled the breakfast table, and headed for the window over the the sink. Mur followed, saying, "Maybe a neighbor's. Mrs. Elmer didn't say a word—" She broke off, staring over Lindy's head. "Now that can't be Fred! But it *is*. One white sock and that crooked star—why, the old dear must be thirty if he's a day. I learned to ride on that horse! When I was about Lindy's age. He belonged to some people named Jones—lived just down the road. So what on earth is he doing *here*? I'll have to write Mrs. Elmer—"

"But he can stay, can't he?" Lindy was begging. "I can learn to ride on him too! I can—"

"No, no, no, forget it, honey, he's too old to work. But you can go out and pet him later—he's a nice old boy and he'd love an apple. For that matter I'd love an apple too—I'll bet the Gravensteins are just ripe on that big tree behind the barn. And we used to get Jonathans from the tree by the Little House. By the way, Scotty, the man who bought the Little House—Walt Thatcher, his name is—has a boy about your age. Probably be in your class at school."

"Oh?" Scotty suddenly felt a gleam of hope, mixed with his usual wariness.

"Any girls?" demanded Lindy.

Mur shook her head. "Just the one boy. Don't know his name. No mother—I think they're divorced."

"Is the dad a farmer or something?" Scotty asked in a careless tone. He wanted to keep the subject going.

"More of an all-purpose hired hand to other farmers, I gather. And he raises chickens. We'll be getting our eggs from there. You can run over and get acquainted later on. But right now—"

"Right now, if Scotty'll *ever* get through eating breakfast," said Lindy, "we're going to start hunting for the Money Room!"

"Oh, no you're not," her mother informed her, rinsing her coffee mug and setting it to drain. "You're going to start unpacking all this litter of cartons and putting your own stuff away and making your beds properly. Because I've got to go to Cedarvale to the office."

"Already?" cried Lindy. "But we just *got* here!"

"Having come with the hopeful notion that I could make us a living where we already owned a house, if I put my back into it—remember? Well, I can't sell any real estate before I know what's for sale, and where it is, and how you get there, and how things are set up in the office, and whether I'm going to get along with the boss, and . . . anyway, I told Mr. Crabb I'd show up by nine and it's eight-thirty now and Cedarvale's nearly ten miles away."

"Oh, zonzer dritchagog!" said Lindy crossly.

"If that's Dobish for 'okay, Mur,' I'll accept it," her mother told her. "For heaven's sake let Gretel finish your cereal so she'll get out from under foot. Scotty, when you've emptied the cartons—"

The phone rang shrilly.

For an instant all three of them just stared at the wall instrument hanging just inside the dining room. Then Mur said, "Who on earth?" and went to answer it.

"Uncle Lyle calling clear from Medford?" hazarded Lindy as Scott took his plate to the sink.

"He doesn't even know this number. I don't know it myself yet. Though I suppose—"

"Sh! Listen."

But their mother's half of the conversation, which consisted mainly of yesses and oh-I-sees, told them nothing except that the caller was a stranger, and doing most of the talking. As Binkie chose this moment to start the loud *cheeeeeeeeeeeep*ing noises that meant he wanted out of his cage, and Lindy began chattering about the new school, Scotty abandoned all effort to hear and began to open cartons.

He was just pushing aside the first empty when his mother

hung up, scribbled something on a notepad, and turned away from the phone, looking puzzled. "Well—maybe it's a good omen," she remarked.

"What is?" chorused her offspring.

"A client. It's eight-thirty in the morning, I haven't even been to the office, and already I've got a client!"

Chiefly to make a polite noise, Scotty said, "They ought to give you a raise. Who is it?"

Mur looked down at her note. "Man with a funny name. Says he used to know Gramp. Dorrit L. Suggs." She glanced up with the sudden grin that made her look exactly like Lindy. "He says just to call him Dorrie."

CHAPTER II

By ten o'clock the emptied cartons were piled on the screened back porch, and their contents distributed through the house: towels in the two bathrooms, extra bedding upstairs; the big chiming clock on the fireplace mantel, with Dad's brass lamp and several leaning towers of books parked on the floor nearby; Mur's painted Mexican mirror and a wastebasket full of shoes in the big ground-floor bedroom; games and school stuff and Scotty's moon and earth globes in the small window-lined sun porch Mur called the Nook; and dishes, forks, spoons, pots, pans, and depressing items like half-bottles of mustard and Worcestershire sauce covering every kitchen surface.

"*Why* do people move?" Scotty groaned, removing a last stack of magazines from the drainboard and starting for the living room.

"We don't have to put all this away. Mur said *she* wanted to," Lindy reminded him. "After she's put paper in the drawers and waxed the shelves."

"We could be good guys and do that part for her. Then at least one room could be cleared by dinnertime." Scotty hated clutter; it made his brains feel scrambled. There'd be another upheaval next week, too, when the few remaining bits of furniture they hadn't sold arrived to be worked in somewhere. He'd be glad to see the TV set—here he was, missing all the *Nova* reruns and that new *Master Builders* series about how they built pyramids and cathedrals and things. And they could really use Dad's big walnut bookcase. Scotty dumped the armful of old *American Architect* journals, which belonged in the bottom shelf of that walnut bookcase, and looked around the living room, wondering where they'd put it when it came. It was going to look funny here, among all these old-fashioned chairs and tables. All their things would. Like people in jeans sidling into a meeting of old gentlemen with gold watch chains and ladies with stiff waved hair. Great-Gramp's furniture, this had been; Mur said the house had hardly been changed from the day he died, in spite of the Elmers having lived here ten years after that. Scotty wondered if it would ever feel like someplace *he* lived.

Well, the furniture was Mur's problem, he thought as he headed back to the kitchen. It was her furniture, inherited from Great-Gramp along with the farm and house and everything else—including all those rumored riches in that rumored Money Room, whatever and wherever it was.

"The drawer paper's on that step stool," he told Lindy. "Did you see where I put the paste wax? It's in a big kind of yellowish—oh, I see it."

"But I don't want to be a good guy and do drawers and

things!" Lindy objected. "I wanna—"

"Half an hour," Scotty told her. Ostentatiously, he set the kitchen timer. "If we're not through by then, we quit."

"Oh, okay." Lindy sighed, reaching for the roll of paper. "Scotty, do *you* think the Money Room could be just a joke?"

"I dunno. That's what Mur said." But it was hard to imagine how the joke got started unless there *was* something to it. Yet how could there be anything to it? "It sort of sounds like a joke."

"But Great-Gramp was awful rich once. Mur said so. He owned a whole department store in Portland—Scott's Emporium. Only it's called Ferry's or something now."

"Ferris's. I know all that, but it doesn't mean he ever had a whole room full of nickels and quarters and dollar bills, noodlehead. People don't keep money in rooms, they keep it in banks. Or they buy stocks and bonds and things. Which is what he did. And then it got to be 1929, and the whole stock market crashed, and there went all his stocks and bonds. And then during the Depression his department store went broke."

"Yeah, and he had a heart attack," said Lindy sadly, closing one drawer and starting on another. "It sounds just like that soap opera thing we used to watch summer before last. But if he was so broke how could he buy the farm? That's what *I* never—"

"He already had the farm. Somebody gave it to him once because they couldn't pay their bill at his store. *You* know." Scotty glanced at Lindy impatiently. "I told you all about it a long time ago—right after Dad died, when Mur kept wishing we could move up here, only the Elmers were here already, with no place to go."

"Well, I didn't care about Great-Gramp then, so I wasn't listening," Lindy explained reasonably. "Now I like him. I like his house. Did you know a man *and a cow* are walking right down the middle of the road, right past our driveway? I saw that same man with that same cow when I first got up, and he was going the *other* way then. Do you s'pose he's just exercising it, or what?"

"I don't think cows need much exercise." Scotty glanced out the big bay window at the man and his cow—big news in the way of traffic for this neighborhood. He opened the next cupboard. "Get busy, a half-hour's not long."

"Okay, if you'll tell me again about Great-Gramp."

So Scotty sighed and told her again, beginning with the months and months it took the old man to recuperate, in both mind and body, from the avalanche of disasters that had hit him. Weak and ill, fed up with money and its worries, everything gone but one small farm, he had been glad enough—for a while—just to sit by the window and rock, and watch without much interest as the Elmers tended cabbages and chickens. But as his strength came back, so did the energy and shrewd business sense that had once built a tiny dry goods store into Scott's Emporium. He began to focus on what he was seeing. Before long, Mrs. Elmer had found herself tending twice as many chickens and gathering three times as many eggs, in a modernized chicken house, and Mr. Elmer was plowing under the cabbage and potato fields, bulldozing a patch of scrub woods, and planting nineteen acres of an outlandish new crop—filberts—on which he was ordered to lavish unheard-of quantities of fertilizer every spring.

"And the next thing you know—well, after a few years,"

Scotty amended, "the place was making it big. Not as big as Scott's Emporium, of course, but big enough, and it got everybody else around here planting filberts too—Great-Gramp was about the first to try 'em." He grinned over his shoulder, momentarily feeling he'd done the whole thing himself. "Pretty good, starting with nothing but a one-horse farm."

"Yeah!" Lindy agreed. "And so then he got rich again and this time he hid all the money in his Money Room, and—"

"No, he didn't ever get rich again, and I don't know where the Money Room comes in, or when. But he never moved back to town, he lived right here, even after Great-Gran died, all the rest of his life until he was ninety."

"Ninety!" Lindy echoed, sounding stunned.

"Ten years ago. I was just three. And you weren't even born. Took another *big* heart attack to kill him," Scotty finished. He could remember his dad saying, *You've got to hand it to the old boy. He was quite a guy.*

A little grudgingly, Scotty did hand it to him. But who was to say Dad couldn't have been quite a guy too and gradually studied his way from contractor to fully licensed architect and maybe built bridges or Civic Centers or even space cities, if he'd had ninety years to spend on it, instead of just a measley thirty-five?

He'd be thirty-eight by now, Scotty reflected. And oh, if *he* was alive—if we'd never even heard of an old yellow pickup with a doped-up driver, if we still lived on Cherry Street and went to our old school and the McBee kids lived right next door—what would we want with any old farm then?

For that matter, what did they want with it now? He

couldn't help wondering as he dragged the step stool over to get at the top shelves.

The new position gave him a view out the window over the sink, and he stood a moment, looking at this unfamiliar landscape that was going to get familiar whether he liked it or not: tangled rose vines, firs, fruit trees, a glimpse of Fred standing motionless in his little pasture, probably sound asleep. You might say this is still a one-horse farm, Scotty thought with a flash of amusement. Judging from what he could see of the filbert orchard, the trees were heavy with nuts—but not as heavy as they should be, according to Mur, who had remarked that the Elmers had obviously got stingy about fertilizer the minute Great-Gramp wasn't there to prod them. Scotty suddenly wondered who was going to harvest all those nuts, with the Elmers gone. How *did* you harvest them?

"I kind of wish Mr. Elmer hadn't died," he said aloud.

"Well, *I* wish he'd died a lot sooner," said Lindy heartlessly. "Then we'd never've had to crowd in with Gramma Holloway and Uncle Lyle, and then move over to Fortieth Street and that *yicky* old school where we didn't know anybody, and then leave *there* and move into the apartment, and—"

"I never knew you minded all that much," said Scotty, pausing to look down at her curiously. It had always seemed to him that Lindy remained cheerfully Lindy whatever happened, generally turning up with a new bosom friend about five minutes after the dust settled.

She set her hands on her hips and stared up at him. "Never knew I minded *Daddy* being killed? Or minded Gramma Holloway talking and talking and *talking* about him till we could hardly stand it, and Uncle Lyle taking *care* of Mur all the time, and bossing us, and making Gretel sleep outdoors when she's *always* slept in my room, and—"

"Oh, well, sure, when we were at Uncle Lyle's. But I mean —on Fortieth Street—"

"Where Binkie caught cold and nearly died because it was so drafty, and that snerkish boy at school ruined the very best drawing I ever made—"

"Okay, I'm sorry," Scotty said contritely. "I just thought—"

"You just thought I don't have any *feelings*. Because I don't go around *moping*."

He was struck by the truth of this—at least, the half-truth. "Yeah, I guess I do tend to sort of. . . ." The sentence trailed off. "I'm sorry," he added.

"Well. Don't let it happen again." Turning back to her labors, Lindy stumbled over Gretel, who was making her sausage-shaped, polished little self extremely obvious underfoot. "What d'ya *want*, Gretel? It isn't anywhere near dinnertime, you just had breakfast! . . . Listen, Scotty, if the Money Room isn't really a room—full of money—then what is it?"

"You're asking *me*?"

"Well, I mean what kind of other things could it be? A secret hidey-hole somewhere, maybe? Or a box, or a . . . let's see . . . shed? Or an old dollhouse? Scotty! A room in a dollhouse! Why, that might—"

"Slow down, slow down, can you see Great-Gramp stuffing twenty-dollar bills in a room in a dollhouse? They're wide open in back."

"Oh, yeah. Well, *you* think of something. Try to imagine."

"I can't even imagine the reason he's supposed to have created this secret whatever-it-is. Or when." Scotty leaned an elbow on the top shelf, rag dangling. "Yeah, *when?* Now that's a good question. Not when he first came out here, 'cause he was flat broke. And not later, because by the time Mur was a little kid the whole Money Room story was just an old family joke." He refolded his rag and began waxing the shelf. "Probably a joke's all it ever was, Lindy. Because it was just after he'd *lost* all his money that he was supposed to have hidden that million or so away."

"He didn't lose it all," Lindy said promptly. "He'd saved some out. Nobody knew it but him, but he had a sack . . . a whole little *airline* bag full of solid gold necklaces and some diamonds and rubies, and a lot of thousand-dollar bills. And he had Mr. Elmer build a little tiny *room* sort of place in the attic or somewhere. . . ."

She went on for quite a while. Scotty smiled, then sighed, recognizing the familiar symptoms of another of Lindy's obsessions. These were usually short-term: I'm going to have the best dollhouse in the block, I'm going to get so I can ride a big girl's bike, I'm going to learn to make meat loaf and chocolate-chip cookies, I'm going to teach Binkie to perch on the hinge of my glasses. But until she achieved them, they tended to be wearing for her friends and family. I'm-going-to-find-the-Money-Room seemed likely to be more wearing than most.

Resigning himself, Scotty waxed and rubbed and listened patiently, until Gretel once more got out of her basket and walked around restlessly on Lindy's feet. "Maybe she needs some water," he suggested—quite inaudibly, since Binkie at that moment launched another *cheeeeeeeeeeep*ing campaign.

"Holy Maloney!" he added. "Can't you make that bird shut up?"

"No, because he wants to get out and fly around, and I'm not supposed to let him. Ha! There goes the timer. End of good-guy stuff. I did all but two drawers. *Gretel,* if you don't —oh, I know! I'll bet she wants water. Oh, poor baby."

Scott, who had finished the shelves, abandoned his rag and wax can and stepped from the kitchen stool up onto the counter itself, picking his way around to the sink to get a better view out of the tall window. "You know, I keep wondering where that famous Little House is. Mur says it's on a half-acre, along with a great big chicken house, but I can't even see the roof."

"Don't step on me, I'm going to fill Gretel's bowl," said Lindy from just below him. "Say, maybe I'll take Binkie upstairs and let him fly around in my room, while I unpack. He couldn't get lost *there.*"

"Might be down by the lane," Scotty said thoughtfully. "Behind all those trees."

"There you are, baby—wow, you *were* thirsty. Come on, Bink, let's go unpack. Scotty, hurry up or we'll waste the whole day without even getting started on the Great Search!"

Scotty lingered a moment, peering across the fenced back yard and the jungly vegetable garden beyond to the edge of the fir grove, which extended downhill alongside the filbert orchard. About halfway down the grassy alley between them, he could see what could be merely a gap in the fringe of weeds and ferns, but *might* be the beginning of a little path, winding secretly into the grove. Maybe it led to the Little House. If so, that Thatcher boy would know all about it. He probably knew this whole place like the palm of his hand. Scotty made a mental note of the gap's relative position before he jumped down from the counter.

Giving an affectionate ear-tousle in passing to Gretel, whose expression plainly told him that, fond as she was of him, she did not at the moment wish to be disturbed, he climbed the steep, narrow stairway to the second floor.

The brain-scrambling effect of his own room wasn't as bad as the kitchen's, but he spent a toilsome half-hour just clearing the first layer and sorting stuff into piles. Deciding where to stow the piles was a bigger problem, what with no bookshelf and no inside-the-window-seat glory hole (like the one in his beloved lost room on Cherry Street) for awkward items like hiking boots and Dad's tools. And no place at all for his most valued possession, a 15"-diameter model of a space city called Starbright, laid out on a sky-blue circle of plywood and covered by a plastic dome originally meant to ripen fruit. Beneath the dome were curving streets and houses like bee-hives and soaring, tilting freeways, all beautifully crafted out of styrofoam and Popsicle sticks by his dad's patient skill and his own devoted but humble assistance. The work was only half complete—brutally halted by an old yellow pickup. Some-day, when he was learning how to be an architect himself, Scotty was going to finish it.

Meanwhile, the dresser top was the only place to display it properly. His comb and brush and jar of pencils and Swiss army knife and snapshot album, which usually lived there, would have to go in a drawer. The lamp could stay.

Scotty made his bed, thrust his clothes into other dresser

drawers (it was a looming Victorian dresser, with carvings and a high dim mirror, rather intimidating) and was standing wondering what to do with all the rest of his belongings when an unholy racket burst out from the lower regions.

For a minute the racket was too complex to diagnose, and he was too surprised to try. Then the door to Lindy's room burst open and he heard her galloping down the stairs, muttering, "Good grief what's got into that dog?" and he realized—to his utter astonishment—that at least part of the noise was the unaccustomed sound of Gretel barking. She never barked—or almost never, not unless she was startled out of her wits into a bout of hysterics and bogus ferocity. Certainly she never made stumbling and clattering sounds accompanied by low moans, and— At this point Lindy, too, began to shriek and yell out orders and make a racket surpassing Gretel's, and Scott came unglued from his spot on the floor and galloped downstairs himself.

A totally unlikely tableau met his eyes in the kitchen. Lindy was down on both knees, restraining Gretel as if she were a dangerous German Shepherd; Gretel was straining into her collar growling curses; both were staring with deep suspicion at a boy who stood in the doorway between kitchen and screened porch, holding a plastic pail and staring warily back at them. He appeared perfectly harmless: a smallish, skinny boy of an age somewhere between Scott's and Lindy's, with a round, freckled face and sandy hair falling over his eyes in a sort of sheep-dog curtain, behind which he seemed to be trying to hide. Scott couldn't blame him in the circumstances, which seemed incomprehensible.

"What's going on?" he demanded of Lindy.

She shrugged without taking her stern gaze off the stranger. "All I know is he was *in* here, and Gretel bit him."

"*Bit* him?" Scotty's jaw dropped as he noticed that the boy's jeans were torn near the ankle of one leg, on which he was standing to rub the ankle with his other foot. "*Gretel* bit him?" he repeated in disbelief.

"Well, *I* didn't!" Lindy retorted.

"Sort of scratched me, is all," the boy said in a high, rather husky voice. "I came in to bring the eggs."

"But Gretel never—" Scotty was beginning, when it hit him. Boy. Eggs. Little House. It was the Thatcher boy. Oh, lord, he thought with a sinking feeling of doom. What a way to start. "Gretel tore your jeans," he said hollowly.

"Naw, that hole was there. She only snapped, but her tooth caught in it, and so I jerked away, and I prob'ly hurt her tooth, and we sort of couldn't get loose from each other for a while. It's okay."

Scotty glared hopelessly at Gretel, who having concluded her performance of sound and fury had now subsided against Lindy's knees, and was regarding the Thatcher boy placidly. "Have you lost your marbles?" Scotty asked her crossly.

"Bret borgan! Unglepumby!" Lindy rapped out. "Zozatuta!"

"Crimeny sakes, talk English," muttered Scotty, his embarrassment now complete. "Or better yet, keep quiet!" he added as with an effort of memory, he translated her remark from the Dobish as "Use caution! Enemy! Tell you later!" He turned back to the victim, his ears on fire. "I'm sure sorry. Gretel never acted like that before."

"Oh, well. I'm used to it." The boy's attention seemed

riveted on Lindy. Without rancor, he added, "They all snap at me."

"They do?" Scotty said stupidly.

"Maybe they don't like freckles. Oh. This here's your dozen eggs." With a wary glance at Gretel—who looked tactfully away—he stepped far enough into the room to set his pail on the counter, then backed away to the doorway again. "I'm to bring 'em Tuesdays and Fridays from now on. My pop says. I'm Barney Thatcher. From down at the Little House."

"Yeah, I . . . my mother mentioned. . . ." Frantically, Scott tried to think of something intelligent to say. "My name's Scott. That's my sister Melinda."

"Yeah," said Barney, whose fascinated gaze had returned to Lindy. "I better go now."

He retreated, still watching Lindy with an unaccountable mixture of alarm and disbelief in his light-lashed, blue-green eyes. Baffled and despairing, Scotty looked at her himself, and for the first time noticed that Binkie was perched in his favorite spot on the right hinge of her glasses, looking like an elaborate yellow eyebrow. Besides that, she had been crouching like a hostile statue during the entire encounter, and, now he thought of it, had spoken as much Dobish as English. No longer puzzled by Barney's anxiety to be gone, Scotty muttered, "So long," and glumly watched his likeliest chance at a new friend vanish out the screen door and probably out of his life, except for ten seconds every Tuesday and Friday. He had no doubt at all that Barney would now tell everybody in the school that the Holloway kids were weirdos, the boy a dummy and his sister a creep, and that their dog bit people.

"Well, between us we sure loused *that* up," he snapped at

Lindy. "Why'd that stupid little scaredy-dog have to go and *attack* the only kid we might've got to know around here?"

"Gretel's *not* stupid," retorted Lindy, releasing her dangerous beast at last and standing up. "There's something *bad* about that boy and she *sensed* it."

"Oh, pig slop. The only thing bad about him is that Gretel never saw him before. I bet he took her by surprise. If she'd seen him coming, she'd have run as far as she could go and done her ferocious watchdog act from behind the couch or somewhere the way she always does. She was probably sacked out, woke up and saw this awful threatening monster trying to leave us some eggs, and just lost her head, that's all." He added crossly, "*You're* no better. Enemy, my foot!"

"You wait and see!" Lindy told him with narrowed eyes.

Scotty stalked back up the stairs without replying. In mutinous silence, Lindy and Binkie followed.

Twenty silent and brooding minutes later, Lindy appeared in the doorway of Scotty's room carrying her two empty suitcases and demanded, "What'm I s'posed to do with these?"

"Mur said there's an attic," Scotty told her shortly. His mind was on the inviting gap he'd seen in the bushes at the edge of the fir grove. Despite all his ingenuity, he had found no home for three stacks of books, his fourth-grade rock collection, and all Dad's woodworking tools including the jigsaw, and he was feeling an immense urge to see the last of these rose-covered walls for a while and get away by himself. As soon as Lindy left he bounded down the stairs and out the door into the sunshine.

A few minutes after that, he had walked from the uphill end of the grove to a spot well past the last tree that could conceivably be seen from the house, without spotting a sign of a gap or anything resembling one. Wondering crossly if too many moving days had addled his brain, he was trudging back up the slope when, for the second time that morning, a wild commotion scattered his wits and turned his legs to jelly. This time it was Lindy, screeching solo, and even from this distance the decibels were alarming. He had already broken into a sprint when she burst from the house and ran wildly into the back yard, screaming, "SCOTTY! Where are you, where are you, WHERE ARE YOU?"

"Here! I'm coming! What's wrong?" he gasped.

"Nothing's wrong! But I've found the MONEY ROOM! *And about a jillion dollars!*"

CHAPTER III

It was not a jillion dollars—though at first glance it looked like it. Arriving breathless at the attic door with Lindy, equally breathless, capering madly around him, Scotty stared across the room at the red tin box open on the floor and knew an instant of pure, exhilarating belief in fairy tales and happy endings and hidden treasure.

Then he went closer. The money didn't seem *green* enough somehow, though otherwise it looked exactly like a mound of ten and twenty dollar bills, the kind with the picture of a building in the center . . . except these weren't tens and twenties. They had a big numeral "one" in each corner. Still panting, as much from excitement as exertion, he stepped close enough to snatch one up, peer at the words under the picture.

"One peso," he read blankly. He turned the bill over, noted the man's portrait at the left side—wrong place on the bill, wrong man—and more words, across the top: "Central Bank of the Philippines." Aloud he exclaimed, "They aren't even dollars, Lindy! They're Philippine pesos."

There was a long silence, filled only by the sound of hard breathing gradually becoming normal. Then Lindy said uncertainly, "We've got a jillion pesos?"

Scotty heard himself give a slightly hysterical giggle. "Maybe half a jillion. But I'll bet they're not worth anything."

"Not *worth* anything? They're *money*, aren't they?"

"Yes, but not all money counts the same. My fourth-grade teacher brought a French banknote to school one day—a 1940 one—and it said 'five hundred francs' on it, but he said it was only worth *five* now—five *francs*—and a franc was only worth about one of our quarters anyhow."

"But how—but why—"

"They just changed the whole system around. The French did. So they wouldn't always have to be subtracting big numbers in their heads to make change. At least, I guess that's why they did it. I know they made one of the new francs equal a hundred of the old ones, just overnight, because my teacher was there when it happened. And then in *England*—"

"I don't want to hear about in England," Lindy said. "I want to find out how many pesos we've got." She hunkered down beside the box and began taking out bills. "What's a peso worth? In cents? Or dollars?"

"I don't know," Scotty admitted. He hunkered down too, noticing the box itself for the first time. It was about the size of a bread box, with a close-fitting lid, much nicked and scratched like the rest of it. It had once held Henderson's Tea Biscuits, according to the fancy, old-fashioned lettering still discernible on the sides—but that was obviously a long time ago.

"Hey, look. They're not all pesos," Lindy said suddenly. She was sitting on the floor, her lap full of one-peso notes and her hands full of some other kind of bills entirely, which she had just taken out of the box. These looked nothing at all like dollars. In spite of their crumpled, ragged state they were plainly bigger and squarer than dollars, and printed only on one side. The lettering was strange and pointy, impossible to read, with the most elaborate, curlicued big capitals Scotty had ever seen, and the bills varied in color—one was mostly brownish, another white and lavender with some of the printing in green. . . . He looked more closely at the big green letters printed over the little black ones. Did that say "million"? No, "millionen." But that must *mean* "million" in some language or other, and the numeral was 20. . . . He flattened the bill out, stared hard at the peculiar-looking letters, and suddenly made out "Ocktober, 1923," then "Banknote," and finally, "Berlin."

"It's German!" he exclaimed. "A German banknote for— Lindy, it looks to me like *twenty million* . . . of whatever they are. It says 'mart' but I thought German money was called 'marks.' Wait, maybe that is a 'k.' The letters are real different from ours."

"Where does it say 'million'?" Lindy asked in an awed whisper.

Scotty showed her, then swapped his white note for the brownish one she was holding. Hers was much harder to read because the letters were all jammed together, but he made out the "millionen" again—and the numeral on this one was

500. Five hundred *million* marks? Even if marks were worth only a penny apiece, that would be five million dollars—that single bill!

"There's a catch in it somewhere. There's bound to be," Scotty muttered. But in spite of all reason he was feeling oddly clenched up inside, and wishing Mur would come home to tell him what all this was. Or how to find out, anyhow. "What else is in that box?" he asked.

There was a drift of other banknotes under the thick layer of marks, from several countries, a few of which he could not identify. "Československo" might be Czechoslovakia, but what about "Magyarország"?

A fitted tray divided the box; under it were a lot of other papers, the kind you'd call "documents," folded in thirds like letters. Several had insurance companies' names across the front fold, and two said "Deed." All the rest were big sheets of stiff, crackly paper that rather *looked* like money, with elaborate pictures at the top showing hefty goddesses pouring fruit out of cornucopias or hugging wheat sheaves—pictures like the ones on banknotes and stamps and in real old books you found stuck away in your Gramma Holloway's upstairs hall in a bookcase with glass doors. Around the edges ran a wide border of spiderwebby figure-eights, surrounding a white rectangle like a check, which had some printing in flowing script and two blank spaces left where a name and number had been handwritten in. The written-in name was always "Pelham Richard Scott," which was Great-Gramp, and the number might be one hundred or fifty or two hundred, and the fancy printing always said the same thing: that Pelham Richard Scott was the owner of that many shares of capital stock in such-and-such a company. There were certificates from half a dozen companies: Amalgamated Freight, Inc., American Steel Corporation, CS&W Railroad, Cascade Pulp and Paper Company, International Fertilizer. . . .

"Are those money too?" Lindy demanded, peering over his shoulder.

"No," Scotty said in tones of deep respect. "But they were sure worth a lot of money once. They're Great-Gramp's stocks and bonds."

"*Those* are? Just that little pile? How d'you know?"

"It *says* on them. Right there—'capital stock.' But he probably had lots more than these."

Lindy studied the pile with dissatisfaction, remarked that she hadn't thought stocksenbonds would look like *that*, and turned back to her pesos and marks. "I like these best. I'm going to count 'em all up. Wow, is Mur ever going to be surprised! That we found the Money Room so fast. *I* was the one who found it, too, so you just—"

"Lindy, this can't be the Money Room. So there's a box of old papers and money in it—probably worthless money—" Clinging hard to common sense, Scotty swept a comprehensive gesture around the room. "So look what all *else* it's got in it too!"

There was certainly a lot else in it. Scotty got up and began exploring. It wasn't a real attic, on top of the whole house in a third story. It was only the space over the kitchen, entered through a door three steps up from the second-story hall—a long, dim, dusky place unfinished except for flooring, with a single tall window in the gable end. It had a skinny brick chimney flue sticking right up through the middle of it, rafters swooping down low on the front side like the roof of a lean-to, and tin can tops nailed here and there on the high back wall, probably to stop up mouse holes. "Junk room" would be a better name, thought Scotty as he went poking about among old cartons, discarded furniture, and shelves full of everything you could name, from a shoebox jammed with out-of-style dress patterns to a fruit jar full of old keys. There was even a row of oil lamps gathering cobwebs on a top shelf, and several battered suitcases, stuck all over with hotel labels, shoved back against the low front wall.

"Great-Gramp must've traveled a lot while he was still rich," Scotty remarked, peering through the shadows in an effort to decipher the labels. But the room's sole window was about the size and shape of an arrow slit in a castle tower, and allowed little light to filter back here under the eaves. Scotty turned away, adding, "I'll bet he brought that foreign money home as souvenirs of trips."

"Maybe some of it." Lindy stood up and dusted her hands triumphantly. "But if you can explain to me what anybody'd want with *seventy-four* souvenirs of the Philippines—all exactly alike!—and a *hundred and eighty* look-alike souvenirs of Germany—"

"Are there that many mark notes?"

"Count 'em yourself! And worth millions and millions and—"

"Lindy, they can't be! They must be fakes or—or play money for some game—or no good because they're out of date—" Scotty broke off as something clicked in his mind. Date. He'd seen 1923 on one note. He crossed the room to pick up another: 1919. A third said 1922. And suddenly he realized social studies was good for something after all. "Lindy, they're inflation marks! We read about 'em in sixth grade. Listen, you remember that movie we saw once on TV, about Germany after World War One, when money got so it wasn't worth anything, and—"

"Oh! The one with the poor little dog? And that mean old—"

"Yeah, that one. And that guy had to bring a whole basket of money to buy one loaf of bread—"

"Yeahhhh," said Lindy, remembering.

"Well, the basket was full of these things." Scotty tossed the marks down. He almost wished he hadn't found the answer, at least not so fast. Then, scoffing at himself, he went back to his prowling. Hidden treasure in an attic! Phooey. "Likely that whole box of stuff isn't worth as much as this!" He held up a very dusty piggy bank and rattled it. It sounded about half-full.

Lindy's hopes, dashed in midstream, changed horses at once. "Scotty! Coins! Whaddya bet they're gold pieces? No kidding —people used to give each other twenty-dollar gold pieces for their birthdays in the olden days! Grandaddy Scott said Great-Gramp gave *him* one whenever—"

"Yes, and he had to turn 'em all in to the bank a long time ago because they got illegal or something."

"But what if Great-Gramp forgot all about that piggy bank full, or—"

Scotty, with an exaggerated sigh—but a small inner stirring in spite of himself—upended the bank and gave it a couple of brisk shakes. A penny dropped to the floor, rolled in a neat circle, and settled. A nickel followed. Another penny. "Satisfied?" he inquired, as much of himself as of Lindy.

"Oh, all right, Mr. Know-it-all. Maybe the pesos are worth something. Anyway, we'll still find the Money Room! This just isn't *it*, that's all. I wish we could talk to somebody really old, don't you? Somebody who was around when Great-Gramp was. . . . What's in all those cartons, did you look? Oh—dishes. And kitchen stuff. We've got too much of that already. . . ."

They spent another ten minutes poking about and getting dusty, at which point Lindy announced that she was now going to take a long, pink, bubbly bath. Scotty lingered to slide back the glass doors of an old oak bookcase very much like the one at Gramma Holloway's. But the few books were mostly collections of sermons and essays and Lord Byron's poetry—nothing about architecture—and all in microscopic print. The jumble filling the rest of the shelves—yellowed newspapers, leather-cornered ledgers, bundles of tattered letters—made him feel sort of old and tired just to look at them and as if he wanted to go outdoors and climb a really difficult tree. With a last glance at the red tin box, now restuffed with its worthless riches, he went out and closed the attic door behind him.

As he passed the bathroom an idea occurred to him. He tapped on the door, called "Hey, Lindy!" and when the splashing paused, went on, "You know what you said about talking to somebody old? How about if I write to Gramma Scott in Washington, D.C.? She was already a grownup when Great-Gramp went broke—she might remember something."

"*Great* idea! Do it right this minute!"

Scotty rather thought it was a great idea himself. But he

had got no further than locating paper and pen when the day's third commotion broke out from downstairs. Gretel again. The move to the farm had evidently convinced her, overnight, that she was a Watchdog, solely responsible for a house, a shed, a barn, and a total of twenty-three acres.

Scotty ran downstairs, hoping against all reason for the egg-boy again—Barney Thatcher. But this time it was an old man standing just inside the kitchen door, ignoring Gretel, who was barking from the safety of her basket next to the stove. He was peering all around the cluttered room and craning his long, wrinkled neck toward the dining room. He was a tall old man, a bit slouched and stooped but not at all feeble-looking, with a thatch of stiff, no-color hair, steel-rimmed glasses, and big knobby hands thrust into each side of his overalls bib.

"Oh. Hi," said Scotty, thinking, We're going to have to put a *hook* on that back screen door.

"Well! Howdy-do, sonny! Howdy-do! Welcome to Dover! I reckon you'd be Mrs. Holloway's youngster." The visitor ambled across the kitchen as if *he* were the owner, his square, ruddy face split in half by a smile full of porcelain teeth, and one of the big hands outstretched.

Scotty reluctantly put his own in it, endured a grip that rasped like a nutmeg grater, and was glad to get his fingers back whole. He admitted he was Scott Holloway.

"Yep, yep, I thought as much. Don't favor your mother, though, way I remember her—short, plump sorta girl, wa'n't she?"

"I look like my father," Scotty said neutrally. He was waiting to be told who this man was, and why he had invited himself straight into the house, and whether he was somebody one was supposed to be nice to. Scotty hoped not—he was already feeling a strong dislike.

"Oh, your father, mm, can't say I ever met your father. Knew your ma, though, when she was just a little squirt, and your grandpa, 'fore he took hisself off back east to Washington, D.C. and stayed there. And I was mighty good friends with your great-grandpa."

"You knew Great-Gramp?" Scotty said, thawing slightly.

"Oh, you bet I did! Him and me were great pals— I was twenty-five year younger'n him, but it din't matter. Used to play pinochle together, him and me. Old son-of-a-gun. Still miss 'im. Suggs is the name, by the way Dorrie Suggs. Oldtimer around these parts. Come to see your ma on a little matter of bi'ness."

"Oh!" exclaimed Scotty, suddenly enlightened. "You were the one that phoned this morning. But I thought—" He went to the telephone, found the pad she had scribbled on. "This says you weren't coming till one o'clock. 'Dorrit L. Suggs, one p.m.' She isn't even home yet."

"Sure, sure, I'm a little early. Don't matter a bit."

"But it's only eleven-thirty," Scotty protested with a dismayed glance at his watch. "I don't know exactly when she'll be here, but—"

"Don't matter a bit, sonny. Scott, is it? They call you Scotty, like your great-grandpa?" The knobby hands were tucked comfortably into the overalls bib again, the steel-rimmed glasses flashed this way and that around the kitchen and over Scott's head toward the rooms beyond. "I'm in no hurry a-tall, young Scotty, I'll just wait. Got back from my lawyer's, over to Oregon City, little sooner'n I expected, and

I just thought I'd come on. . . ." The glasses flashed down at Scotty, along with an expanse of the too-perfect teeth, as Suggs began to amble about, apparently aimlessly, talking as he went. "Be a pleasure to look around the old place again. Don't think I been here since *old* Scotty died—your great-grandpa, I mean. But I used to come every Satiddy evening, for that pinochle game, regular as clockwork, then he'd come to me on Tuesdays."

"Mr. Suggs, I think it might be better if you came back at one o'clock," Scotty said as firmly as he could without actually being rude. He had to turn as he said it, because his unwelcome guest was slouching right past him, into the dining room. Scotty followed, managing, with some difficulty, to get in his way near the living-room door. "I mean we just barely moved in. You can see we're in kind of a mess, and—"

"Oh, mess don't bother me a-tall," Suggs assured him with his broadest smile, stepping around him and walking into the living room. The glasses flashed everywhere. "My land, you ought to see *my* room sometimes, when my daughter's been too busy to come in and kinda swamp it out. I'm not much of a housekeeper. . . . This here a kinda sun parlor, or what?"

He was in the Nook, looking around sharply, as if he'd never been this far before. Scotty bet he'd never been farther than the kitchen. Maybe than the yard. He couldn't believe Great-Gramp had ever been a pal of this nosey old big-mouth.

"Mr. Suggs, even when my mother *does* come home, we'll have to have lunch. And after that—"

"Oh, I'm not a-going to take up more'n a minute of her time, young Scotty. Not more'n a minute. Won't delay your lunch two cents worth. Whereabouts was that stair, now, led up to the top story? Oh, it's that door next the dining room, innit? Been so long—"

Scotty, who had been momentarily relieved to see him turn back toward the kitchen, now felt something like panic. He hurried after the old man, whose long legs seemed as efficient as seven-league boots for transporting him instantaneously from here to there. "Mr. Suggs, *wait* a minute! *Please!*" He reached the stair door first by half a second, and flung himself against it, arms outstretched, feeling as silly as a soap-opera heroine, but also as angry as he'd ever been in his life. "You can't go *up* there!" he cried, glaring straight through Suggs's glasses into the eyes behind. "It's not your house, and besides, my sister's taking a bath!"

"Why, I'm not a-going to disturb her, sonny—wouldn't dream of it! Just wanted to have a little look around the old place—"

The eyes behind the glasses were like gray pebbles—if pebbles could ever be said to twinkle jovially, without actually changing expression at all. Suggs was reaching for the door knob. He seemed perfectly capable of simply shoving Scotty aside and going upstairs. Scotty had his mouth open to yell *I won't let you!* when to his infinite relief he heard the bang of the screen door, and his mother's voice saying, "Scotty? Whose car is that in the. . . . Oh."

She had arrived in the kitchen doorway—and though Suggs leaped back pretty smartly for a man his age, Scotty was sure she had taken in the whole soap-opera tableau. Her eyes had gone very cool as they ran over the stranger.

"This is Dorrit L. Suggs, Mur," Scotty explained disgustedly. "He came early." With grim satisfaction he dropped down onto the breakfast-nook window seat to watch his mother take over.

She said not a word for quite a while. It was neither necessary nor possible, since Dorrit L. Suggs was doing all the talking. Scotty heard a replay of the whole old-pals-with-Great-Gramp-Satiddy-night-pinochle-game routine, plus a lot more old-timer stuff, and watched the glasses flash and the toothy smile split the face, and the big hands nestle like ungainly kittens in the overalls bib. And he watched, with an admiration that grew into a desire to cheer hilariously, as his mother stood unmoved, impassive and silent.

Eventually, even Dorrit L. Suggs ran down, though he gave not the slightest hint of suspecting that he was not as welcome as summer rain. When he was quiet, Mur said pleasantly, "Did you have some business to discuss with me?"

"I did! I did an' all! And I think you might be a little surprised, when we set down to talk about it." The gray pebbles twinkled at her.

She made no move to sit down. She merely said, "Suppose you tell me what it is."

Scotty longed to screech with laughter. He yearned for Lindy to be there with him, watching, deadpan. Not that old Suggs would have noticed if they'd been rolling on the floor. Old Suggs was eyeing Mur, and he had gone quite still, though his smile was still in place. It occurred to Scotty that Dorrit L. Suggs might not be as homespun and thick-headed as he acted —and that he was finding out Mrs. Janet Scott Holloway was a little brighter than he'd thought.

"Why, I can tell you in two words what it is," he said jovially. "I want to buy this house."

Scotty could feel his face go all saggy with surprise, and when he quit staring at old Suggs to flash a glance at his mother, he saw the same expression on hers.

"Buy *this* house?" she echoed. "But whatever made you think it was for sale?"

"The price I'm willing to offer," answered old Suggs simply. He removed a hand from the overalls bib, forced it partway into a pocket that looked entirely too small to accommodate it, and fished out a slip of paper. He handed it to Mur.

She looked at it blankly, handed it back. "But I'm not at all interested in selling. At any price. Why, we only just got here!"

"Sure, sure, not even dug in yet, I can see that." Old Suggs smiled around the cluttered room, glasses flashing. "Makes it that much easier to pull up stakes and move on—if you stop to think about it."

"But. . . ." Mur gaped a moment at this reasoning, then waved it aside as not worth comment—with Scotty's silent but hearty approval. "Well, the house is not for sale. Frankly, I can't imagine what you want with it—a man your age—and a widower, I think you said."

"Oh, I always did like the old place," old Suggs said easily. "I'm a little crowded, over to my daughter's—kinda like to spread out some. Had my eye on the proppity for some time, tell you the truth. If I'd of known how to reach you, I'd of made my offer before you came clear up here, but—"

"Well, you've made it now, and I've refused it." Mur moved pointedly toward the kitchen door. "And I've plenty to do before evening, so if you don't mind—"

"All rightee, we'll just leave it for the time bein'. But you think it over." Old Suggs slouched toward the doorway too, his smile undimmed, his manner confident as ever. "You might want to change your mind."

The screen door slammed. Scotty and his mother stood bemused, listening as his car started up outside and slowly crunched along the graveled drive toward the road.

"Who *was* that?" demanded an affronted voice.

Scotty turned to find Lindy standing at the foot of the stairs with the same expression of baffled outrage he could feel on his own face. Obviously she had arrived in time to get a strong whiff of Dorrit L. Suggs's personality. Scotty told her who it was, then turned uneasily to his mother.

"You won't change your mind, will you?"

"Of course not. The man must be batty—and what a cast-iron nerve! Did he just walk right in?"

"He's not the only one!" began Lindy. "There was a—"

Scotty broke in. "Hey, Mur, d'you know what Gretel did? She—"

"Shut up, *I'm* telling her. Oh! We found the Money Room, Mur, at least we thought we did, only—"

Gradually, in bits and pieces, their mother heard the tale of their eventful morning.

CHAPTER IV

To Scotty's somewhat gloomy satisfaction—for this was one time he'd have loved to be wrong—Mur confirmed all his suspicions about the treasure in the attic. The German banknotes could be nothing but the notorious post-World War I inflation marks, she agreed as she examined them with fascinated eyes. The mixed foreign bills were of value only as souvenirs. As for the pesos, a phone call to a coin dealer's shop established their total worth at thirty-seven dollars even in 1931—the most recent date on any of them—and by this time they would bring exactly nine dollars and ninety-nine cents.

Just how Great-Gramp had come by so many Philippine pesos remained a small mystery (Lindy at once invented a homesick Filipino gratefully repaying Great-Gramp for a loan that got him back to Manila), but why he had never bothered to bank the pesos was plain enough. In 1931 he had been ill, soured on the world, self-exiled to this farm with his back turned on money dealings of any kind; anyway, thirty-seven dollars would have seemed chicken feed after his millions. It was easy, Scott thought, to imagine him stuffing those pesos into the old tin biscuit box along with the worthless certificates and shoving the whole thing out of sight. For all the documents were worthless, Mur said—the deeds both nullified, the insurance policies on cars and houses long since sold, and the stock in companies that no longer existed.

Lindy asked, and received, permission to use the entire contents of the box as play money, and that was that.

It was nearly three weeks before any of the Holloways thought of the Money Room again. On Monday school began, and the all-too-familiar pattern of knowing nobody, nothing—not even which classrooms were which—began again for Scotty. This time it was worse than usual, since he and Lindy were the only newcomers in a school where everybody else seemed to have been pals in their playpens, or were actually related. Every second name he heard seemed to be Schubert, Wrenowski or Baxter, unless it was Jones, Chavers or Kuhn.

"You won't believe this," Lindy announced as they walked in from the bus that afternoon, "but I've got two Jack Baxters and one George Baxter in my room—all cousins—and a Jackie Chavers and a Georgia Wrenowski and a George Jones, *and* a teacher named Miss Kuhn."

Scotty, feeling like a released prisoner after the lurching roundabout ride sitting like a stick among a busload of chattering old friends, believed it without difficulty. So did Mur, for different reasons.

"Sure, those families have been here forever," she told Lindy. "I played with kids named Chavers and Baxter and Jones when I was your age and used to come visiting Gran and

Gramp. Lots of small towns are like that—anyway these old farming communities like Dover. Quite a bit of the land around here actually still belongs to descendants of the original settlers who came out here in the 1840s and claimed it."

"In covered wagons?" said Lindy, staring.

"In covered wagons. And on foot."

Scotty tried hard to find this fascinating, and did, in theory. In practice, it only meant this school was going to be twice as hard as usual to break into—or so it seemed to him.

Not to Lindy. The next afternoon she marched in from the bus with an air of triumph and a new friend in tow—a wispy girl about her own age, with a waiflike face and a halo of thin pale hair that looked as if one good puff would send it flying like dandelion fuzz.

"Where's Mur?" Lindy demanded of Scotty, who had elected to walk home today.

"Previewing a listing—other side of Cedarvale. She just phoned."

Lindy scowled, then philosophically accepted Scotty as second-best recipient of her news. "This is Carol Jane Jones," she announced, adding wistfully, "Isn't she *skinny?*"

Since Scotty could not deny bald truth, but strongly suspected—judging by his own experience—that this was not the compliment Carol Jane most liked to hear, he was left effectively tongue-tied. Fortunately Lindy didn't wait for an answer.

"And you know that old horse, Fred, and Mur said he belonged to some Joneses that used to live right up the road? Well, those were Carol Jane's grandparents! And now Fred belongs to Carol Jane's folks, and they *still* live right up the road, and the reason he's in that pasture is because the Elmers always let him be there and eat the grass, and Carol Jane and I are going out to the pasture right now as soon as we get something to eat, and she's going to teach me how to curry Fred, and we're going to be best friends. Aren't we, Carol Jane?"

Carol Jane, who had stood passive and expressionless throughout this speech, her pale blue eyes on Scotty, now glanced at Lindy, smiled a wide, sudden smile, and said, "Yeah."

"So do you want peanut butter or cheese with your crackers?" said Lindy cozily as they turned away.

Lindy, as always, had landed on her feet.

Scotty could only envy her. Through the next week, as he doggedly sorted out his classrooms and subjects, he struggled through the mire of new-school agonies, weighed down by his accustomed certainty that he was already being labeled either "dumb" or "stuck-up" by everybody who saw him, for the very good reason that he was acting either dumb or stuck-up. He just didn't know how to quit.

It started the very first day with the usual barrage of side-long, careless glances as everybody—*everybody*—examined him minutely while pretending they didn't even know he was there. Naturally, he had to pretend he didn't know they were there either. *Stuck-up.* He could practically hear them thinking it.

And after lunch—at which he had disgraced himself by asking for a milk glass when at this school you were supposed to drink it from the carton—he had been unable to find the library. It was supposed to be Room 101, but wasn't, he found when he got there. He was forced to ask a class-mate where it was.

"Right here. You're in it," the boy said, staring at him. It was somebody-or-other Chavers, the oldest of three brothers much in evidence around the school, all black-haired with broad grins, given to exchanging cryptic shouts with the nearest Baxter or Wrenowski, over other people's heads.

"*This* is the library?" Scotty looked around at what appeared to be an ordinary classroom except—he now saw—for low bookshelves running all along three walls, and some tables in the far end. He heard a snicker behind him, and the Chavers grin appeared in front. *Dumb*, they were thinking.

"Whadja have where *you* came from, the whole liberry a Congress?" murmured a voice he failed to identify, being busy muttering something himself and making for the book shelves with his head down. The tone of the voice came through loud and clear, though. Dumb *and* stuck-up, they were all now deciding—*thinks he's so big-town and Dover's Nowheresville and we're a bunch of hicks.*

Well, maybe it is and maybe you are, he thought furiously, blinking through a fog of humiliation at a row of book spines he couldn't focus on until his cheeks cooled. When he did form some idea of the library's scope and range, his heart sank like a stone. No use expecting to find new information on architecture or buildings or cities or the pyramids or space colonies or anything else he liked to read about, not here. He could only hope there was a library in Cedarvale.

Barney Thatcher was not in his grade, but Scotty caught sight of him several times that first day—once from the bus

window, pedaling a battered red bike toward school, later in
P.E. watching Scotty miss his third basket in a row and then
ducking away behind his sheepdog fringe as if trying to be
invisible. At lunch Scotty spotted him two ahead in the line,
but before he could speak, Barney had grabbed his tray and
hurried off to the farthest table.

Okay, if that's the way he wants it, that's the way it'll be,
thought Scotty, pointedly turning the opposite way.

As he sat chewing his sawdust sandwich at a table of ebul-
lient Old Settlers he asked himself what else he had expected.
Maybe we wouldn't have got along anyhow, he told himself
stolidly, wondering why he had ever imagined there might be
somebody at the Little House who was just a little like Donnie
McBee.

On Wednesday the surviving Holloway furniture arrived
from Medford, including the TV set and Scotty's bike, with
which he had a joyful reunion from the moment he came from
school until Mur's expert two-fingered whistle dragged him
home to dinner. Coming down the road from north of the
house, he wheeled in bouncily over the old rutted barnyard
entrance and spotted Lindy on her way from the pasture to
the house. He dismounted and joined her, walking the bike.
She and Carol Jane had spent a heady afternoon communing
with Fred, and she was bursting with things to tell him about
horses and curry combs and fetlocks and withers and botflies,
but he had a few things to tell her, too.

"I found out where the Little House is," he reported when
she finally ran down. "It's way down over *that* way, past the
bottom of the filbert orchard and on along the lane almost

to the Colby road. I rode about two or three miles the other way, too—I mean north, up this road. I saw where Carol Jane lives—they've got a mailbox with robins painted on it. And right next to them, some of those Wrenowskis have a big holly orchard, and there's a Baxter across the road, and right behind *us*—other side of the creek—is a Chavers. I think it's where those three black-haired Chavers boys live. The ones that grin all the time."

"Did you know you were s'posed to keep a horse's feet clean?" Lindy demanded. "You take a little stick and scrape all around inside their hoof—first you have to pick the foot *up* and sort of hold it on your lap. They don't mind at all. Carol Jane did it."

"I'm going to ride my bike to school after this," remarked Scotty, propping it against the shabby, paint-thirsty siding of the screened back porch. "Then I can explore around Dover, too. Someplace different every day."

"And not ride the *bus?*" exclaimed Lindy, her attention finally captured. "But it's so much fun!"

"Not for me! I'd rather be on my own."

Lindy was at once uneasy. "But what if I need to ask you something? Or tell you I'm going over to Carol Jane's? Or—"

"You can just write a note, can't you?" said Scotty. He was officially in charge until Mur got home, and Lindy always needed to feel she could put her hand on him if necessary. She seldom did so, but the need was real, as Scotty was well aware from moments like this, when she was abruptly anxious for no reason. It didn't take Mur's careful little grownup-to-grownup talks to make him understand that for Lindy he was a kind of half-baked substitute for Dad—one so ludicrously inadequate, in his own opinion, that he couldn't help feeling for her.

"Well—okay."

Reluctantly she dropped the subject, but only until bedtime, when Scotty had forgotten all about it. Just as he was slamming shut his math book she appeared in his doorway, pajama-clad, waving her toothbrush and apparently foaming slightly at the mouth with the brilliance of a new idea.

"*Now* I've got it worked out! We'll *each* write a note! Every day! Because listen, Scotty, if you're not going to ride the bus we'll be leaving at different times in the mornings and getting home different times, and there's bound to be stuff we really *need* to let each other know about, like new clues about the Money Room, or—"

"We're at the same school all day," Scotty reminded her. "We could—"

"No! That'd be boring. We'll leave regular notes, in some special place, like—well, somewhere real secret. And here's the best thing—we'll write them in *code*."

"Code? What code?"

"The one you're going to make up," Lindy told him exuberantly, and thrust her toothbrush back into her mouth.

"Oh, Holy Maloney." Scott sighed, but he couldn't help laughing at her, standing there scrubbing her teeth in the hallway, watching him with bright, expectant eyes—and as usual, he ended up nodding. It might be sort of fun, he told himself, to work out some kind of code, just to see if he could.

"I'll see what they've got about it in that dumb library," he told her.

By the next afternoon, with the help of a little-kid's book

he found, he had devised a simple cipher, easy enough to work with but pleasingly baffling in effect. When he came home, after a short bike tour of the main streets of Dover, he tossed a coded message onto the kitchen table, where Lindy and Binkie were sharing crackers and jam.

"Already?" she gasped. She stared at the note, which read: NOODN STEEO HEEWU ISOCR RSCOT, then raised her eyes to Scotty with an expression of such awe that he felt like an imposter.

"I didn't actually—" he was beginning, when she cut in on him.

"What does it mean?" How do you work it? Show me!"

He slid in beside her, rescuing the last two crackers from Binkie, who fluttered away to the safety of Lindy's glasses, protested deafeningly for twenty seconds, then in an injured undertone began running through his entire vocabulary: *Binkie-boy, pretty Binkie* (sometimes *pretty Scotty*), *Mur, dirty bird, nightie-night*.

"You shouldn't give him jam," Scotty told his sister for the fortieth time as he ate the crackers himself. He reached for his school notebook.

"Well, but he likes it," Lindy replied, also for the fortieth time. "What are you doing?"

"I'm drawing a big triangle," Scotty mumbled with his mouth full. "And now I'm going to draw five lines across it like this, and five lines down, starting from the first crossing line, so it's divided into a lot of little squares in the middle, with a triangle at the top and triangles and polygons along each side. Like that."

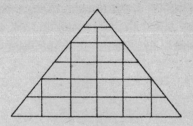

"Gotcha."

"Then *you're* going to write a message in it—first letter at the top, next two in the two spaces below, and so on—left to right, just the way you normally write. It'll have to be a short message—twenty-three letters or under." He tore the page free and handed it to her.

"Okay." Lindy groped for the pencil, meditating, then wrote. "I've got spaces left over. Does that matter?"

"No, just put in nulls. The first couple letters of your name, or any old thing. Now copy those letters off in a line an ordinary sentence, only start with the letter in the *bottom* left space, and work upwards—and whenever you get to the top of a column go to the bottom of the next one and take that letter, and so on. But save the letter in the very top of the triangle to put *last*." He waited with his back turned while Lindy scribbled industriously. "Okay. Now divide those letters into groups of five, as if they were words. If they don't come out even, put in more nulls. . . . Okay, give it here."

The message read OJUAA ESNRT OEEOO NLSLC IHGPZ. Scott drew another triangle, copied the letters back onto its squares beginning with the O in the lower left corner and working up, just as Lindy had copied them off of hers.

Then he read it aloud, left to right, in the normal fashion: "GONE TO CAROL JANES HOUSE LI. And of course I'd understand the L and I and that PZ on the end were just fill-ins."

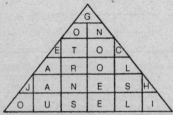

OJUAAESNRTOEEOONCLSLHG

OJUAA ESNRT OEEOO NLSLC IHGPZ

GONE TO CAROL JANES HOUSE LI

"I get it, I get it, I get it! Oh, it's *great*, Scotty, how'd you ever think of it?"

That starry-eyed look again. Scotty said, "Oh, Lindy, I *didn't*. I mean I found a lot of ciphers in that book, and I just sort of adapted one."

The uncritical admiration in Lindy's face dimmed to a look of resignation. "There you go again. Why won't you ever take the credit? I'd never have known the difference!"

"Well, but it wouldn't have been *so*." Scotty got up to find the cracker carton, wondering how Lindy could always make him feel sheepish about just acting honest. "I did invent the *adaptation*. But—oh, never mind. I Cannot Tell A Lie."

"That's one of your problems, all right," Lindy agreed and settled down to decode his note.

CHAPTER V

After some discussion, they decided on the potato cellar as the official message-leaving place. It seemed more suitable than the barn, being much farther from the road and any possible curious passerby. "And much more inconvenient for us," Scotty pointed out helpfully.

"Who cares? Think of the *privacy*. Nobody would ever come here except on purpose."

"You're so right." Standing on the splintery old ramp tilting up to the shed's doorway, Scotty glanced diagonally back across the stretch of rough ground between him and the house —a weed-grown no-man's-land with the fruit orchard and Fred's pasture on one side, and the barn with its big yard giving onto the road on the other. When the rains started, they would probably need hip boots to get out here. Oh well. If he knew Lindy, the note-leaving craze would last about as long as her jogging-to-school craze a year ago.

Leaving tomorrow's problems for tomorrow, he followed

Lindy on up the ramp and through one half-open—in fact, unclosable—leaf of the sagging double doors. He had not been inside the shed before, and he now saw that it was even more dilapidated than it looked. It was windowless, but who needed windows, he asked himself reasonably, as he noticed the daylight streaming freely between the shrunken boards of the walls, and a patch of blue sky visible through the rotting roof. The place was completely empty except for some old planks lying at one side and a big pile of burlap sacks smelling of mildew that looked undisturbed for years.

"Why did they call it a potato *cellar?*" he asked Lindy.

"Because there's a cellar underneath." Lindy pointed to the floor of heavy twelve-inch boards, the sturdiest part of the building. "They only used this part for machinery and stuff, Carol Jane said—they stored the potatoes in the cellar part. Come on, I'll show you."

She led him outdoors again, down the ramp, and around the building, which was perched high on its cement foundation. At the back, a short flight of steps led down to a wooden door opening into the cellar—a low, dark, dirt-floored room actually only half underground, the top half being enclosed by the five-foot-high foundation. It, too, was empty, except for a powerful earthy odor, not unpleasant, which Scotty privately labeled "ghost of potato."

"So where do we leave the notes? The middle of the floor?" he inquired.

But even brief association with Carol Jane had made Lindy an authority on the farm buildings. She led him through the gloom toward a side wall, where he now perceived some rough shelves—holding nothing but an ancient ball of twine firmly anchored to its corner by ancient cobwebs—and a tall, narrow cupboard. It was a type that might have started life in somebody's kitchen, though years of outdoor damp had made it look almost like part of the earthen wall. But its begrimed and peeling doors still opened—complainingly—and the rusted latches had been replaced by hand-whittled wooden tabs that turned on nails.

"We'll leave the notes in these two little drawers," said Lindy triumphantly. She had opened the top pair of doors to reveal a couple of cutlery-sized drawers, and was digging in various pockets. "Where's the code stuff, that piece of notebook paper we were writing on? Did I drop it?"

"Probably left it in the kitchen."

"I *didn't*. I put it right in my shirt pocket so I'd be sure not to forget how to. . . . Oh, well. Pretend I've got a message in my hand, okay? Now I've strolled out here real casual, as if I'd just come out to get some potatoes or something, and before I come inside I look *all* around—moving just my eyes—then I duck in real quick and run over here and stick the message in your drawer and close it and run back, and a minute later I'm strolling away as if I'd never even come in after all." Slightly flushed from her exertions—she had acted everything out in mini-drama—she turned to Scotty with sparkling eyes. "Nobody'll *ever* catch on we're leaving notes here."

Scotty solemnly agreed, thinking privately that if any of Lindy's imaginary spies *were* lurking around, such behavior was guaranteed to make them suspicious.

"So. Left-hand drawer for your notes, right-hand for mine." Lindy latched the cupboard doors and dusted her hands with satisfaction. "Now you *promise* you'll check that left-hand drawer *every* afternoon?"

Scotty promised, mentally giving the whole thing about two weeks.

Before the first week was over he had made a discovery of his own, not much farther from the house but in the other direction. Shortly before noon on Sunday, idly searching for the mushrooms his mother said used to grow along the edge of the fir grove, he suddenly spotted the gap in the bushes he had noticed that first day from the kitchen window. It was neatly camouflaged, to anyone at ground level, by a tangle of wild rose vines hung now with only a few dry leaves and the little red-orange rose hips—like tiny footballs with the stuffing coming out one end. In a season of full foliage and blossom he would never have seen the gap even from the window.

It was just what he'd suspected, the beginning of a path into the grove—much wider once, but narrowed now to a barely discernible track through the encroaching ferns and salal. It looked as if no one had used it in years. All the better, all the more private and special, thought Scotty, whose ideas along these lines differed considerably from Lindy's. It was cooler in here among the tall trees, and dim, and still, except for the quiet brush of the wind through the branches far overhead, and occasional small scuttlings through the ferns below. The layer of fir needles and moss and compost underfoot felt like a thick, springy carpet, and it smelled mysterious and wonderful, not at all like the sunshiny country smell among the weeds outside.

The path meandered around huge rotting stumps and

clumps of vine maple and occasional upthrust boulders, sloping always downhill, and there was so much to notice and admire that it was a wonder Scotty saw the arrowhead at all. But his eye was suddenly caught by a glint of white under the edge of a long-fallen log, and when he stooped to look, there it was: small, perfect, businesslike—just like the ones in museum cases.

It seemed a lucky sign—the only one he'd had since they'd moved to Dover—in fact the first he remembered in the past three difficult years. And it was immediately proved so, for as he raised his eyes from it he saw, across the log and a little way off the path, a patch of green so emeraldlike that he clambered over obstacles and through a screen of red huckleberry to investigate it.

He found himself in a little mossy room, encircled by tree trunks and walled by ferns and maple, with another fallen log across one side of it. The patch of emerald edging the other side was a different sort of moss, clothing and cradling some tumbled rocks overhung by a kind of fern with thin black patent-leather-looking stems and fronds of lacy delicacy. The rocks looked wet. They were wet, Scott discovered when he went closer; so was the emerald moss, which squelched under his feet. And once he stood still, he heard the voice of the place—a soft, continuous burbling whose source he finally located among the wettest rocks, a smooth fat welling of water from the brown sand. A spring. A hidden spring. It seeped away through the mosses and rocks to find its tiny way somehow, Scotty supposed, to the creek that bounded the Scott farm along the northeast.

He felt as if somebody had given him a marvelous and

totally unexpected present. He moved slowly, savoringly, across the little room—*his* secret, private room—and sat down on the fallen log to look around him and memorize every spray of red huckleberry, every tree trunk and fern frond, every leaf of the low, green, shamrocklike plant that grew in swathes and drifts between the trees. The Place of the Arrowhead. Indians must have camped here once—maybe lived right here on this farm, when it was all forest like this. Sitting there quiet on his moss-cushioned log, Scotty began to see the Indians almost as clearly as the bushes and ferns. They were a small but proud tribe called the Tillicumclaws, and the name of their chief was Mucklechuk.

By the time he heard Mur's whistled summons to lunch it seemed to come from a hundred miles—maybe a hundred years—away.

He told nobody about his discovery. He could not keep it all for himself forever, he knew that. But for now, the knowledge of it waiting there, secret, perfect, entirely his own, was like a kind of inner armor as he lived his outer life in the unfriendly school, the unfamiliar town, and his alien rose-covered room.

By their second week on the farm, the days had settled into a pattern, beginning with the hollow *clank-plonk, clankety-plonk* sounds soon after seven as the still-unidentified man led his cow up the road. After that came the morning rush of dressing, eating, animal-feeding, sandwich-assembling, and three separate exits from the house. Lindy left first, flying out to the school bus; shortly afterwards the station wagon crunched out the gravel drive, Mur tooting goodbye as she turned in the direction of Cedarvale, ten miles away. And finally Scotty trotted out to the potato cellar to stuff the obligatory coded note in the top drawer, giving Lindy some un-newsworthy message that he usually had to rack his brain to invent. Then he too departed, on his bike.

School absorbed most of the day, and there was no change there: Schuberts, Wrenowskis, Baxters, Chaverses, Kuhns, and Joneses arrived together on the bus, stuck together through the day, and climbed back on the bus together at four o'clock. At 4:05 Scotty headed for the bike stand, first making sure Barney's old red bike was gone. It always was; Barney seemed always in a hurry, and by the time Scotty got home on egg-delivery days the eggs were there and Barney gone. Now and then Scotty glimpsed him pedaling along the lane, or cutting across the Wrenowskis' stubble field beyond the creek; never any closer. At school both of them avoided all contact. Again: no change.

Everybody might as well carry signs saying Keep Out, This Means You, reflected Scotty bitterly.

He took some comfort in the familiar company of his bike, exploring some new area every afternoon. When he finally turned homeward, along the road that seemed so empty and faceless after Medford's lively streets, he rode in by the barn track and bumpily out to the potato cellar to collect the coded note from the left-hand drawer before wandering into the house, walking his bike and deciphering as he went. Lindy's messages were more exclamatory than his but not much more exciting. GONE TO CAROL JANES BEWARE, IN PASTURE BOTFLY EMERGENCY, and AT IMPORTANT

BLUEBIRD MEETING were typical, only occasionally varied by MUR PHONED WILL BE LATE or GRETELS FOOT HURT LOOK.

Until Thursday of that second week. Thursday's message read: MEET ME BIG STUMP URGENT. Scotty frowned at it, a little puzzled but mostly irritated. It was a hot, still afternoon, and he had biked farther than he'd meant to. He wanted nothing so much as to make a huge peanut-butter-and-pickle sandwich and disappear with it and his tattered copy of *Young Architect's Handbook* to the Place of the Arrowhead. However, Lindy might have been waiting quite a while already. He detoured by the Gravenstein tree for a couple of apples and headed for the bottom of the filbert orchard, where the huge old blackberry-twined stump of some long-gone oak or walnut marked the edge of the lane.

Lindy wasn't there; there was no sign she'd been there yet.

He waited in the sun, standing on one foot and then the other, growing hotter and tireder and more impatient, until he'd finished both apples. Then he sat down on an uncomfortable tentacle of the stump's root and waited a few minutes more. He then flung himself to his feet and started angrily up the hill. He'd gone about halfway when he saw Lindy hurrying down, scowling, waving a paper.

"Whaddya *want?*" she called as soon as she was in earshot. "I don't have *time* to come clear down here, I'm busy with Fred's hoof-cleaning!"

"What do *I* want?" Scotty puffed indignantly. "This wasn't *my* idea, don't you think I've got better things to do than—"

"Well, this is *your* note!" retorted Lindy.

They came together, both flushed and glaring, prickling with heat and resentment. Then Scotty captured the paper she was flapping at him, stared at it, and dug in his pocket for the one he'd found waiting in the left-hand drawer. They were identical.

"Where did you get this? When?" he demanded.

"In the right-hand drawer, of course. Just a minute ago. I had to wait for Carol Jane to go home before I could check the . . . why?"

Scotty showed her the notes. "Somebody's playing tricks on us," he said flatly.

A drabness came over the day, a sourness, a kind of sullen misery. He stuffed the notes in his pocket and started for the house, stiff-jawed with trying not to show it hurt. Into his mind came the black-haired Chavers boys, broad grins in place. And whichever Wrenowski lived beyond Joneses. And the Baxter across the road from them. He was surrounded by Old Settlers. Any of whom might have found the code paper Lindy had lost that day, and all of whom were as familiar with the Scott place and its outbuildings as Carol Jane, he had no doubt. Evidently Lindy's spies weren't so imaginary. Even more evidently, they weren't content to keep him out—they were going to intrude.

CHAPTER VI

◆

That was the last hot day, and the last bright one for a while. As if to accord with Scotty's mood, Friday dawned dark and clammy, and—as if to rub it in—all weekend the rain poured down, causing Mur to make an anxious remark or two about the filbert harvest.

"Never mind the filberts, what about my Bluebird picnic tomorrow?" Lindy demanded, staring crossly out the streaming window.

"Oh, it'll clear off tomorrow—just in time for school," Scotty predicted—quite accurately. On Monday there were blue skies full of scudding clouds, with enough wind to dry things off for a slightly soggy picnic. By Tuesday, though it was chilly and gray again, the mud was firm.

It was Tuesday, just about dusk, that the next thing happened. Mur was finishing dinner preparations, Scotty was clearing his homework off the table to make way for knives and forks, and Lindy was attempting to get Binkie back in his cage. This usually involved finding him first, as it did to-night. He was, as Lindy frequently remarked with mingled pride and irritation, a very smart bird, also pigheaded. When he preferred to remain out of his cage he simply rendered himself invisible, a motionless, pale blob in some obscure corner behind a chair leg or high on a drapery rod, and he was capable of holding his pose until long after Lindy had run out of patience. Tonight she discovered him on the inner frame of a lampshade in the dusk-filled living room and switched on the lamp as she began her usual scolding. This broke off at once, and Scotty heard her give a dismayed exclamation.

"Oh, Mur! He's gone and binked this lampshade!"

Mur heaved a sigh and went on stirring the gravy. Scotty came in to assess the damage. Binkie's favorite hobby when out of his cage was taking neat, triangular bites out of whatever he chanced to perch on or next to. There was never a maga-zine or newspaper in the house without a sawtooth edge precisely resembling, Mur had once remarked, the edge of a fabric "pinked" with pinking shears. Her children in chorus had transposed the term to "binked." All three of them had learned to keep business or homework papers well out of sight, guard any cardboard box they wanted to keep, and watch out for possible new ideas from their enterprising bird, whom Scotty had once found perched on the edge of his li-brary book, busily binking the very page he was reading.

Now, it seemed, he had begun on lampshades.

"Well, he can't do much harm," Lindy said hastily, starting for the kitchen with the culprit between her cupped hands. "That lampshade's not just paper, it's something real tough."

"His beak's tough too," Scotty reminded her, looking with

misgiving at the neat bites scattered around the upper edge of the parchment shade, through which the wire frame showed.

"And most of them *are* just paper," Mur added. "If that's going to be Binkie's new kick, I warn you, Lindy, I'm going to ground him. Come to the table, you two."

"But if he has to stay in his cage he'll *screech*," Lindy protested. "And besides—"

It was then that a sudden sharp report rang through the dusk outside.

Scotty and his mother exchanged a startled look. "What was *that*?" demanded Scotty, and Mur said, "Was that a gunshot?"

Lindy, who had got as far as the sink on her way to Binkie's cage, was staring out the window. "I saw somebody!" she shrieked. "Running out of the potato shed! At least I *think* it was somebody."

Scotty and his mother jostled each other getting to her side. But there was nobody and nothing to see now except the shed with its doorway concealed by the half-open door, and a corner of the barn to the west and the backdrop of fruit trees to the east—all barely visible, for it was nearly dark.

"*I* don't see anybody. You probably imagined it," Scotty told her.

"I didn't! I saw *something*—just a kind of fast shadow. Maybe it went into the fruit trees." Lindy popped Binkie into his cage and turned to her mother. "*Honest* I'm not making it up. Only it was gone so quick—"

"I believe you, honey. But I doubt if it was Bad Guys." Mur's voice was resolutely calm. "A bird flying into the trees could have looked just like that, this time of evening. Come on, let's sit down, everything's getting cold."

"But Mur—the gunshot!" Scotty protested.

"It might not have been that at all. I spoke without thinking. If it was, then one of our neighbors is out potting gophers in his lawn, or graydiggers in his orchard, or rats in his barn, or starlings in the holly trees. There's a dozen good reasons for gunshots in the country. Come and eat dinner!"

"You don't think I ought to—go check up?" Scotty said uncertainly. He suspected his mother was being brave for their benefit, and he felt dimly that *he* ought to be, for hers.

She looked at him thoughtfully a moment, then reached for the flashlight they kept on top of the refrigerator. "Come on. We'll all go."

They took Gretel with them, but Mur vetoed Scotty's suggestion that he take Mr. Elmer's old shotgun, still in its rack over the kitchen door, saying it was more likely to explode in his face than terrify intruders.

"Not that we'll find any, or even a sign of one," she assured them both.

Her prediction was not quite accurate. Both shed and cellar were empty, but pervaded by a distinct smell of exploded gunpowder. They stood sniffing uneasily as Mur's flashlight played over the deserted, unexciting interiors of both underground and over-ground levels. Gretel sneezed, but seemed otherwise unimpressed.

"Neighbor kids, maybe," Mur said in her most prosaic tone.

There seemed no other explanation that made any sense at all, and nothing more to be done. They went back in the house and ate dinner.

But first thing next morning, before they'd even had breakfast, Scotty and Lindy headed by common consent for the potato cellar. Daylight revealed the shed unchanged and as uninformative as before; even the gunpowder smell was gone thanks to the copious ventilation. But a whiff still lingered in the cellar below, and in a shadowy corner of the dirt floor, Scotty suddenly spotted a scrap of red. He leaped for it, picked it up, then held it out to Lindy with an angry tightening of his lips. It was instantly recognizable—the red paper from a firecracker.

"Our fun-loving neighbors again," he said.

"The ones that tricked us with those notes?" Lindy's eyes opened wide; her braids appeared to curl up on the ends from sheer indignation. "Well, of all the snerkish, unglepumby. . . . What was the *point* of it? They're stupid along with everything else!"

"Yes, they are. Wanted to scare us, I suppose. But they scared Mur, too. I could tell." Encountering Lindy's startled glance, he added quickly, "Just sort of worried her, I mean— made her wonder if somebody was prowling around."

Lindy didn't look at all reassured. "Scotty—suppose somebody *is*."

"No. Mur's just—well, she's used to the city, with somebody right in the next apartment or even in the same house. Here she's—on her own. It's pretty different for her."

"She's got us. And Gretel!" Lindy said staunchly.

Scotty nodded, but he doubted if his mother placed much reliance on Gretel's new role as ferocious watchdog. Or much on him, either. In fact, it was the other way around, with everybody in the family, animal, bird, or human, relying entirely on Mur. "I wish I were older!" he muttered.

For an instant Lindy looked as if she wished he were too, but then she said, "Well, you will be, if you just wait. Let's go back, I'm starving." Turning as she spoke, she automatically glanced toward the cupboard, and stopped in surprise. "Hey—was that cupboard door open like that last night?"

"I don't know. No—it wasn't! Mur shined the flashlight on it and both the tabs were latched."

"That's what I thought too!" Lindy pulled the door farther open, opened the right-hand drawer, pushed it shut, opened the left one, and pounced on a folded note. "Ah-*ha!*"

Scotty was beside her, bumping heads to get a look at it. DLHGE AUTAE IYARW RRLEB, it said.

"But we *changed* the code after those other notes!" Lindy was wailing. "How'd he—or they—or whoever it is—catch onto our *new* system?"

"This might be the old one still. Wait'll I try." Scotty fished a pencil stub from his pocket and used the bottom of the note to decode. A moment later he said, "It's the old one. BEWARE TALL GUY RED HAIR. Phooey. Just part of the big joke."

"Yeah, I guess so." Lindy glanced at him uneasily. "But I *did* see somebody run out of that shed. I'm *sure* it wasn't a bird." Her eyes widened, began to sparkle. "Scotty, maybe we've got a friend! Somebody on *our* side, not the one who left those other notes! This note's from a mysterious, secret friend who wants to warn us about this tall red-haired man who's prowling around here and—"

"Oh, Lindy, come on. Why doesn't he just walk up to the back door and knock, then, and tell us? Or walk right *in* the way everybody else seems to do around here."

"Because the red-haired man would clobber him, that's why! He's scared to reveal his identity like that. He's going to keep clear out of sight and just *spy* for us, until—"

"Until what?"

"Well—till the mystery's solved."

"*What* mystery?"

Lindy scowled at him a minute, then whirled and started for the door. "Oh, I think you're *mean*. *I* don't know what mystery—if I did, it wouldn't be one, would it? Can *you* explain whoever—or whatever—I saw running? Or who left this note?"

"Well—I think it's those Chaverses, playing tricks," Scotty told her gently. He followed her over the rough ground toward the house, rather sorry he had ruined her fun, and wondering if she really was nervous about some imaginary red-haired prowler. "Tell you what, Lin. Let's leave a note ourselves this morning. We'll just say 'who are you?' If it's a friend, he'll tell us. He wouldn't be scared to reveal his identity in a secret note, would he? And if it's the Chaverses, they'll just pull some other trick."

Lindy considered, forgave him, and enthusiastically agreed. They put the note in the left-hand drawer before they went to school.

Unfortunately, all that week it rained again—not hard, but continuously enough to discourage anybody's visits to the potato cellar, even their own. There was no use expecting an answer from the "mysterious friend" for a while. Meanwhile—just in case, Lindy said—they kept a sharp lookout for a tall, red-haired man—or even a big red-haired boy, for as Scotty pointed out, "guy" didn't necessarily mean "adult."

But there was neither boy nor man of that description at school. A casual questioning of Carol Jane turned up no local character who fit the bill, nor were there any among the now-familiar regulars who drove past on the road, morning and afternoon. Even the drizzly streets of Cedarvale, when Mur took the whole family to the dentist on Wednesday, offered mere blonds and brunettes, all middle-sized, plus one auburn-haired child about four years old.

Scotty found no red-haired guys in Dover, either, though disregarding the showers he combed the entire downtown section—a grid of five streets comprising about seven square blocks—wandering damply in and out of the drugstore, the cleaners, the grocery, the lumberyard, the hardware store, checking every clerk and customer.

Leaving the post office Friday afternoon he got a jolt of surprise as behind him, he heard the postmaster say, "That's Miz Holloway's boy just goin' out the door, Henry. That tousle-headed kid." Scotty turned, clawing self-consciously at his cowlicks, and saw stumping toward him a wizened, weathered little man who reminded him of a twist of rusty barbed wire. The man bobbed his head in greeting.

"Name's Baxter, son," he said, predictably. "Henry Baxter. I'm the fella leases your ma's filbert orchard. Tell 'er I'll be around fust thing Monday morning with m'flail—if it don't rain me out. Knock down the last of them weeds. Once this cold spell lets up—'f it ever does—nuts gonna be comin' down fast. I'll be there eight sharp. Don't fergit to tell 'er."

Scotty hastily promised not to fail, and conscious of several pairs of eyes now curiously scrutinizing Miz Holloway's tousle-headed kid, he turned away so quickly that he nearly knocked over a dumpling-shaped old lady with a mole on her chin, who was just hobbling in, leaning on her cane. Mumbling apologies and receiving a vague but amiable response, he escaped, feeling as though his face were on fire.

Next morning he went out to check his private postbox, but the note inviting the "mysterious friend" to reveal himself remained unanswered, gathering cobwebs in the drawer—though by now it had been dry enough for several days to make access to the potato cellar easy. Scotty told himself stolidly that he'd expected nothing else. He waited one more day. Then on Sunday afternoon he removed the note and angrily tore it up.

"It was just a dumb, stupid trick," he informed Lindy. "I told you. There's no tall red-haired man or boy in this part of the country, far as I can see. But there's three dumb, stupid black-haired Chaverses right across our creek—as handy to that cellar as we are."

Lindy was doubtful. "Yes, but it wasn't dumb and stupid to figure out our code—unless they found the same library book you used. But that Chavers kid in my class *never* reads a book. I don't think he knows the library's there."

"So they got somebody else to do the brain work. Or got hold of that piece of paper you lost that day—it had the whole code right on it." Scotty shrugged hopelessly. "Anybody could've found it. That Wrenowski who lives across from Carol Jane. Or the egg-kid."

"Barney *Thatcher*? He wouldn't know what a code is, I bet. Anyhow, you said he lives half a mile in the other direction!"

"Oh, well, what's the difference who did it? They've had

their fun now, ruining our little message-game. Maybe they'll lay off."

"You mean we're going to let them stop us? *No,* Scotty! D'you want 'em to think they *won?*"

Scott hesitated. He would have been delighted to end the message game. But when she put it that way. . . . "Okay, I'll try to think of something."

"Yeah, something they'll *never* figure out!" Lindy's eyes snapped. "Spaghetti-headed snerks! We'll show 'em!"

She marched vengefully away to take a bubble bath. Scotty wandered off to the fir grove and ducked behind the rose-hip curtain to his secret path, trying unsuccessfully to work up some small enthusiasm for fighting back, turning the tricks on the tricksters. It was no use; even trying only made him feel more than ever an outsider, an exile from the place he belonged. It occurred to him that he might always feel that way. Maybe there was just a limit to the times you could start over—and once you reached it, you slid back to square one and never really, inside you, moved again. Maybe you felt displaced forever.

Climbing over the fallen log and edging carefully through the red huckleberry and maple that screened the Council Chamber, he stooped for a ritual mouthful of the spring's ice-cold water, then took his place on Chief Mucklechuk's rather soggy mossy seat and tried to lose himself in the voice of the water, the peace of the ferns and emerald moss, the imagined doings of that proud, small tribe, the Tillicumclaws.

But today it somehow didn't work. He was still seeing Chavers grins, not the Tillicumclaws, and that was all wrong—

you were supposed to leave your troubles at the door of this place, like cowpokes checking their guns at the door of the saloon. He left in only a few minutes, anxious not to dilute the strength of the magic with his unwanted companions. The Place of the Arrowhead was the only thing he really loved in his new life—he couldn't afford to spoil it.

The next morning at eight sharp—Lindy had just climbed on the school bus—Scotty heard the clatter of a tractor from the direction of the orchard and turned guiltily to his mother, who was clearing the breakfast table.

"Oh, hey, I was supposed to tell you that man would be here. The guy that leases the orchard. One of those Wrenowskis or Baxters or—"

"Henry Baxter," said his mother. "*You* were to tell me? Where did you run into him?"

Scotty explained, belatedly delivering the rest of the message and adding, "What's a flail, anyway?"

"A thing he drags behind the tractor—it mows the weeds close, so the nuts have a nice smooth surface to fall on, then the picking machine can do a good job. The nuts are a little late coming down this year—been kind of cold for them," she added, looking out the window at another bright, but chilly, day. "But one good wind would bring them down like hail. Then if the weather will just hold—"

"Can't you pick them in the rain?"

"Hand-pickers can—that's the way Great-Gramp always did it. Took a lot longer. But I'm told you can't get hand-pickers any more. And those picking machines tend to bog down—or *break* down—just as they're getting good and started, and sit there rusting away, while the nuts get soggier and soggier, until the next dry spell. Which might be a couple weeks coming." Mur glanced at Scotty with her quick Lindy-grin. "All of a sudden I'm an authority. I'm only quoting Henry—but he *is* one. He owns a picking machine. Harvests half the orchards around here."

"Will he still be flailing when I get home from school?" Scotty asked, trying to catch sight of the tractor out the window.

"I doubt it. If you want to watch awhile, better do it on your way." His mother rinsed the last cereal bowl, put it in the drainer, and leaned beside him. After a moment she heaved a sigh that seemed to come from her toes. "Let's just hope we get a good harvest. We're going to need it."

Scotty turned to study her profile. "Aren't we—doing so well? I mean your job?"

It was a moment before she answered. Then she gave a brief, unconvincing laugh and said, "Oh, don't listen to me on Monday morning. I'm just cross because I had to spend *another* Sunday afternoon holding an open house and didn't get a thing done around here. We'll be okay. I've got a couple of clients on the string now—not that I'm likely to find anything to suit them. Probably why I've fallen heir to them—nobody else wanted them."

"But—that's not fair!" said Scotty.

"It's normal, though. The new girl around an office always has a rocky time of it for a while. I'm in a cut-throat business, Scott. Sometimes I let it get me down. Don't worry about it." She straightened briskly. "Go comb your hair. I've got to get moving—my day to have floor duty. See you about five—

unless I'm busy writing up some half-million-dollar listing that just happened to fall into my lap first thing this morning!"

"Okay," murmured Scotty. Uneasily, he watched her gather up handbag, briefcase, lunch sack, and head for the car. It struck him she was looking awfully tired.

At slightly after five that afternoon he wheeled bumpily into the back yard from the direction of the barn to see Lindy standing beside the pump house watching Gretel watch a hole in the ground. Gretel was rigid with attention; Lindy merely looked impermanent. She turned, spied Scotty, and instantly semaphored an urgent command for silence, adding a lot of pointing toward the house and drive. Scotty obediently leaned his bike against the rose-padded fence and sneaked across the grass, peering toward the drive, in which stood an old Pontiac sedan, once dark blue, now purple with oxidation and age.

"Who's here?" he whispered when he was close enough, but at that moment he heard a well-remembered voice that answered his question, and the screen door was pushed open to reveal Dorrit L. Suggs, all smiles and flashing glasses, bidding a cordial farewell to a much-less-than-cordial Mur, whose expression of civility looked pasted on.

"You think it over," Suggs was advising her heartily, giving Scotty the strong feeling that this was where he'd come in. "You might change your mind. Offer's open. Any time. I'll be right here." With a jaunty salute he turned away, thrusting the big hands into his overalls bib, and spied Scotty and Lindy watching from the pump house. "Well, well! Howdy there, young Scotty! How's the world treatin' you? That your sister? Mighty pretty little lady!"

The two of them looked at him woodenly, responsive as Egyptian mummies. Suggs twinkled, glanced back at their mother and murmured, "A little shy," then sauntered to his car.

Scotty almost hooted with laughter in spite of himself—Lindy was about as shy as a used-car salesman. But a glance at his mother quenched his amusement. She was leaning against the door jamb watching the purple Pontiac crawl around the graveled circle near the garage, and she looked far more tired than she had that morning.

"Come on," said Lindy as the Pontiac crunched away down the drive. "We can go in the house now."

"How long has he been here?" Scotty asked his mother as he went past.

"I'm not sure. I got here about fifteen minutes ago—found him wandering in from the barn."

"Is he still trying to buy this house—in *spite* of what you said?"

"Yes and no." Mur followed him into the kitchen, reached wearily for the coffeepot. "He's upped his offer. Now he wants to buy the whole farm."

CHAPTER VII

◆

"There's no getting around it," Lindy insisted. "He knows something we don't. About the Money Room."

"Or thinks he does," Scotty amended.

"What he knows," said their mother, "is that this is one of the best pieces of property around here. Orchard drains perfectly, well pumps two hundred gallons a minute, nice old house, fourteen trees full of fruit. . . ." Her voice trailed off wistfully.

Scotty wrinkled his forehead at her. "You think he wants to *farm* the place? Himself?"

"No. No, of course I don't." Mur pushed her coffee cup away and leaned back against the padded seat encircling the breakfast table, where they had gathered to discuss Suggs's latest surprise package. "He wants to resell when the time is right and make a killing. I find he's famous around here for buying up good farms and then just letting them go to pot while he waits for prices to go up. You know that filbert orchard just beyond the old bridge on the Cedarvale road? All weeds and suckers? Well, that's one of old Dorrie's. Used to be a top-notch orchard, Henry Baxter told me."

"Dumb!" pronounced Lindy scornfully. "Who does he think would *buy* a farm like that?"

"Developers."

"Oh!" said Scotty, enlightened. Then his forehead wrinkled again. "But in *Dover*? Shopping centers and condominiums and things?"

His mother's sudden grin made her look much younger and less tired for a minute. "Dorrie's counting on Dover becoming a mini-metropolis in his lifetime. It'll have to hurry—he's seventy-five if he's a day. But Evan—my boss—says the old coot's been buying land around here for ten years—sometimes under other names, using a cousin or somebody as a front. Nobody knows how he keeps up the taxes on all that property, much less the payments. But one way or another he manages." Her smile faded as she shrugged. "Maybe he's on to a sure thing. Sometimes I think the whole world's going to end up solid condominiums."

They sat glumly a moment, contemplating this unattractive vision. Then Lindy shook her head until her braids whipped. "That's not why he's hanging around *us*. He didn't even want our land at first—just the house. He's trying to buy the Money Room, that's what—if he's got to buy the whole farm to get it! Just *think* how much money there must be around here somewhere, hidden away! If we could only find it!"

"Lindy. . . ." said her mother, then gave up, exchanging a private smile with Scotty as she rose and took her coffee cup to the sink. "Okay, you find it, honey-child. I guarantee I'll make good use of it! Right now I'm going to get dinner, and Scott's going out to pick me some plums, and you'd better feed Gretel."

"Okay." Lindy scooted around the curved seat, got the dog food can out of the refrigerator, then suddenly detoured to hug her mother around the waist. "You haven't called me honey-child for *ages*."

"I'm going to start calling you *money*-child if you don't watch out," her mother retorted, returning the hug before sending her on her way with a little shove. "Scotty, take that little plastic bucket for the plums. You want potatoes or noodles with your pork chop?"

Scotty said, "Noodles," and followed Lindy out into the yard, picking up the plastic bucket on his way.

"Listen, Scotty," she said at once, as they walked together along the narrow brick walk. "Let's search this place next weekend. Really *hunt*. We'll have all day Saturday while Mur's at work—and she'll probably have to be in charge of one of those open houses all Sunday afternoon. We can take the house apart!"

"She'll love that."

"Well, we'll put it back together before she gets home. And if we don't find anything in the house, we'll search the barn and the pump house and—"

"Lindy, talk sense! What d'you think we'd find in the pump house?"

"Well, you never know." Glancing at the little building, Lindy added, "Gretel's *convinced* there's something *under* it. Look there—she's still watching that hole." Retrieving Gretel's bowl from a flower bed, she began coaxing her single-minded little friend to take time off for nourishment, while Scotty headed for the gate. "Will you do it, though?" she called after him. "Help me do a *thorough* search next weekend?"

"Oh, all right. But I want to watch *Master Builders* at nine." It wasn't Scotty's idea of how to spend a Saturday—but then, it was just another Saturday. I have no previous engagements, he reflected wryly. And it might get the Money Room off Lindy's mind, so she'll get off *my* back.

It was not just another Saturday. It was a day when everything started changing, though he did not realize it until much later. The search began as soon as *Master Builders* ended and Mur was safely off the premises. Scotty filled Gretel's water dish, Lindy let Binkie out for his morning fly-around, then they headed upstairs to start methodically at the top and work their way down.

"Because otherwise we'll miss something," Scotty said. Having decided to do the job, he was now determined to leave no cranny unexamined. "Think of all the places there are to look! The attic alone'll take half the day. All those old suitcases and bookcases—and that old chimney—"

"We're going to tear down the chimney?" Lindy said with awe.

"We can pull out a brick or two—they're loose. You want to do a thorough job, don't you?"

"Yeah." Lindy relinquished her claim to leadership and became an enthusiastic follower. "Hey, we can peek under the wallpaper in my closet—it's kind of loose in one corner. And I think I know how to get under the house. . . ."

As Scotty had predicated, the attic took half the day, and would have taken longer if he had not continually prodded

Lindy away from fascinating discoveries.

"Look, Scotty! A whole box of old *salesbooks* from Great-Gramp's department store. 'Scott's Emporium.' Why *ever* do you s'pose he kept those? They'd be great to play store with, they've got those little carbon sheets and everything. And you could play bank with the pesos and stocksenbonds! I'm gonna bring Carol Jane up here and—"

"Lindy, come *on*. Help me go through this bookcase."

But Scotty, too, found himself lingering over some of the old papers and ledgers in the bookcase—the very ones he had turned away from impatiently before. There was a yellowed front page of a newspaper dated Tuesday, October 29th, 1929, with huge black headlines announcing the crash of the stock market, and quite a packet of clippings from the next few weeks. There were old letters, among them three from his own mother to Great-Gramp, signed "Janet" in round, childish handwriting and sending love and x's to Fred and to Foxy—another horse? Maybe a dog. The ledgers were only old department store stuff from 1930, but there was one thin leather-bound book that was a sort of diary, full of thin, sloping handwriting in brownish old ink that Scotty was sure must be Great-Gramp's. He had just confirmed this from a reference to "my tenant John Elmer" when Lindy said pointedly, "Scotty, come *on*. Help me go through these bureau drawers!" With a grin, Scotty tucked the diary in his pocket and got back to work.

They found no more money of any kind in the attic, though Scotty did wiggle a brick or two loose from the old disused flue and gingerly thrust in a hand to feel around the sooty interior. He even pried off the can lids over the mouse holes—

and nailed them back again—and painstakingly shook out every unexciting coin from the piggy bank to make sure none were gold pieces. Lindy discovered some old-fashioned clothes in a trunk, which delighted her almost as much as a hoard of dollars would have, but by eleven-thirty or so she was willing to quit trying on Great-Gran's helmetlike hats and pronounce the attic searched.

There was little to explore in their bedrooms, which they knew pretty well by this time, though Lindy insisted on peeking under the loose corner of her closet wallpaper and loosening a corner in her bedroom just to see if Great-Gramp had papered the walls with his millions. Not to be outdone, Scotty slipped the point of his knife under an inconspicuous edge of his tiresome roses, reflecting that if there was anything better underneath he'd simply tear the rose paper off. But there were lilacs underneath, in a die-away, insipid lavender, which was a good deal worse. No millions. The bathroom and linen closet were equally unrewarding—and that was the end of the second floor. The searchers descended to the first and collapsed over a peanut butter sandwich.

After lunch they tackled the lower floor, beginning with their mother's bedroom closet, which was tucked under the slope of the stairway and looked promising, especially way back in the dark, low-ceilinged corner. Disappointed there, they worked their way through the other rooms, from the Nook, with its low bookshelves and windowed walls, to the screened back porch. Here Lindy, kicking aside a square of loose linoleum that seemed to have no purpose, casually stepped forward and put a foot straight through the floor. Only a feat of acrobatics and Scotty's quick supporting hand saved the rest of her from following.

"*Ho-ly Ma-lon-ey*," Scotty breathed when they had re-treated to firm ground and stood looking at the splintered hole in the floor. "We're not going to be able to put *that* back together again."

"I didn't mean to!" Lindy wailed, rubbing her skinned ankle. "I was only trying to see if there was a t-trap door or something under that thing. It *couldn't* have been all my fault —there must've been a broken place already!"

"Yeah, bound to. Probably why that scrap of linoleum was there. Something was sitting on top of it, wasn't it?"

Lindy nodded unhappily. "That old whatever-it-is." She waved toward an ancient washstand full of empty jelly jars, which they had pulled away from the corner earlier. "Could we just put it all back like it was?" she added hopefully.

"We better not." Scotty was testing the boards around the bad spot, and finding them oddly spongy. "Mur ought to know, I think."

"Take a look through that hole, while you're close enough," urged Lindy, always practical. As Scotty gave her an exasper-ated glance, she added, "Well, now it's *there*, we might as well see if there's anything underneath!"

Resignedly Scotty lowered himself to a prone position, put his eye to the broken spot for a moment, then backed away and clambered to his feet. "There is," he informed her. "Cob-webs and a musty smell—and a couple of feet down, the ground. Come on, we've still got all the other buildings to check."

Doggedly, they went on with their search. The potato cel-lar they knew too well to bother with—and there was too little to know. But they looked carefully in the pump house for signs of a secret cupboard concealed behind the cobwebby fruit jars and old kerosene cans ranged along the head-high shelf, while Gretel, who had come outdoors with them, made her own somewhat cursory check of the hole under the side of the little building, in which she seemed to be losing interest.

"I think the rats have moved, thank goodness," said Lindy. "Or whatever they were."

Apparently Gretel agreed, for after a final contemptuous sneeze she came along to the barn, waddling and struggling valiantly across the rough ground on her short little legs and having to be boosted up the final ramp into the vast, dusky interior. There she recovered her poise and trotted about over the heavy, worn boards, sniffing officiously, while her companions wandered along behind.

It was a huge shadowy place, the barn, full of eyebrow-level partitions and high, dim lofts and rather daunting dark corners, with a lot of unidentifiable farm equipment lying around in the way like rusty dinosaur bones. Even Carol Jane and Lindy had not fully explored the barn, but Scotty and Lindy did so now, warily at first, then with increasing interest as their eyes became accustomed to the gloom and their nostrils to the still-distinct scent of the place—a mixture of dust and hay and grain and departed cows, with overtones of milk and mice, that as Lindy commented, sort of grew on you. There were grain bins and a row of stalls and a sort of room in which a heavy old scale with a bar and sliding weights still stood. Hanging on the rough boards of one wall, which was striped with diamond-bright slits of daylight, was a twist of leather reins, its loops hard as iron. With some difficulty Scott climbed a wall ladder minus half its rungs and peered cautiously around the cavernous gloom of a loft, but there was nothing there but strands of hay and a busy wasp nest near the loading door in the rear. When he descended, Lindy was examining with every sign of delight a dirt-encrusted cereal bowl in a corner near the stalls.

"Just look!" she said dotingly. "There must have been barn cats—and they were fed right here, at milking time!"

"Only I don't think Great-Gramp had any cows," Scotty said as he led the way on toward the rear of the barn.

"Mr. Elmer must've, then. I can still *smell* cow. Where are you going, is there a back door?"

"Must be—there's light coming from somewhere back here. Oh, hey! Look at *this*."

It was another little room, with a horseshoe nailed over the doorway and a window large enough to light the sturdy old workbench built against the wall underneath. Scotty stared in growing delight, feeling that the whole day had suddenly become worthwhile. There were clips for tools above the workbench and an old vise fastened to one corner and a bin nearly full of wood scraps. There were shelves to hold glue and nails. It was perfect. He could bring Dad's tools out here and be in business.

"This is going to be *my* workshop," he told Lindy. Rather anxiously, he added, "You and Carol Jane won't want it, will you? You have the attic."

"No, what would we do *here?*" Lindy said with a disdain that made him feel lighthearted again at once. "Come on, let's go search someplace else."

"Where else is there?" Suddenly impatient with the whole

procedure, Scotty followed her to the barn's rear door and jumped the three feet to the ground—the steps had apparently vanished with the years. "This is getting silly. Great-Gramp wouldn't have stashed away any millions anywhere but in a bank! Let's call it quits—we're not going to find any Money Room."

"Well, not today anyhow," Lindy admitted grudgingly. She waved a hand toward the familiar station wagon parked in the drive. "Mur's home."

"Already?" Scotty gaped in dismay at his watch. Four-thirty. And he'd meant to spend half the afternoon in Chief Mucklechuk's mossy Council Chamber, reading that diary of Great-Gramp's he'd found in the attic. Tomorrow it would probably rain, and the moss would turn into a soaked sponge. . . . But in that case, he thought with a sudden little lift of his spirits, I can take Dad's tools out to the workshop and put them in those little clips, and then maybe. . . . His planning was interrupted by a desperate-sounding bark from far behind.

"Oh, poor Gretel, she can't jump down that high step!" exclaimed Lindy. "Go ahead, I'll rescue her," she added self-lessly—and so quickly that she was on her way back to the barn before Scotty realized that it was now he who would be explaining to their mother that hole in the porch floor.

When he came in, Mur was leaning against the kitchen door-jamb looking at it, arms folded, already in her jeans and shirt as if she'd been home quite a while. But her expression was not angry, only rather forlorn. For some reason it struck Scotty that she was quite a *small* woman—an idea that had never occurred to him before. He peered down at his pant legs to see if he'd grown taller without noticing, but they were the same length as always and anyway he knew that wasn't it. It was more as if she was just *feeling* smaller, as she stood looking at that splintered floor.

"I'm sorry, Mur," he said unhappily. "Lindy was hunting for a trap door under that piece of linoleum—that table thing was standing on it, and—"

"It's all right, Scott. I assume she wasn't hurt?"

"Just skinned her ankle a little. How come it just—*gave* like that? She wasn't jumping or anything."

"It's dry rot. Pretty well advanced. And not just in that corner, I'm very much afraid. I've been on a tour of inspection." Mur raised her eyes with something of her normal astringent manner. "What on earth have you two been up to? The place looks as if a cyclone hit it—and then tried to reverse its path afterwards."

"Trying to find the Money Room," Scotty mumbled. He met her glance and shrugged. "Well, I thought Lindy might leave me alone if we made a real job of it."

"You made a real job of it, all right. Was it Binkie's idea to take the paper off Lindy's bedroom walls, or did you start it for him?"

"Oh, Holy Maloney," Scott sighed.

"Never mind, I got him back in his cage. But he's had a high old time binking the edges of everything in sight, and that north corner of Lindy's room is a mess. The two of you are going upstairs pretty soon with some glue and the vacuum. Where is she?"

"Here I am," said Lindy meekly, slipping wary-eyed in the

screen door. "Are you awful cross about the hole? Can't it be fixed?"

"The hole can. The problem can't, I'm afraid."

"There's a—problem?"

"There is. A large one." Mur studied them both a moment in a way that made Scotty extremely uneasy, then seemed to come to a decision. She turned away to the kitchen. "Come sit down. I'd better level with you."

With strong reluctance, Scotty followed her to the table and slid in beside Lindy. He didn't especially want to be leveled with, he realized—not about a problem that made Mur's shoulders go tense and her voice go flat—a large problem that couldn't be fixed. He heard about it anyway. Its name was dry rot, and it was not only serious but infectious, like measles. Mur would have to get somebody out right away, next week, to make a real inspection.

"Which I should have done in the first place," she added as if it were an effort to get the words out. "Before pulling up roots and moving us all up here. I knew better. I just didn't care." She met both pairs of eyes, appealing. "I wanted to come so bad! And it seemed such a good plan. Sensible! House already ours, a little income from the filberts—even a job opening!"

"It *was* good and sensible—wasn't it?" Lindy's voice wavered.

"Except that we've been here a solid month and I haven't sold so much as a doghouse."

Scotty watched her anxiously, feeling his stomach tighten. "But that won't last long—will it? Why, back home you sold stuff all the time!" He corrected himself swiftly. "Back in Medford, I mean."

Mur gave him one of her X-ray glances. "You don't have to pussyfoot, Scott. I know Medford's still 'home' to you. I suppose it is to both of you."

"Not me! I like it here!" Lindy said.

"Well, I'm glad I didn't blow it completely." Mur smiled, but that seemed an effort too. "I only hope we can stay here. I love this old place—you know that. But I was counting on its being rent-free *and* bringing in some filbert money while I got underway in my job. Now, if I've got to *spend* money on it— a bigger chunk than I'll have all at once for years—" She took a long breath and finished in a rush. "Well, it's just not going to work. I'll have to sell it after all."

There was a startled silence, broken only by the sounds of Binkie having a heated argument with his mirror. Then Lindy said in a shocked voice, "You mean—to old Dorrie?"

Her mother merely shrugged. She seemed absorbed in studying a hangnail.

Scotty was astonished at how revolted he felt. "Maybe there'd be some other buyer," he muttered. He found he didn't really care for that thought, either. He couldn't get a grip on any of this—it was too sudden. "Do you mean move back to Medford?"

"No, just into Cedarvale—find a smaller house, closer to the office, so I could come out ahead." Mur threw him an unhappy glance. "It would mean another change of schools."

It was Scotty's turn to shrug. He couldn't feel it would be a hardship to leave this school full of Baxters and Chaverses and Wrenowskis. That wasn't the problem.

What *was* the problem? Something was bothering him more and more.

"Anyway, now you know the worst," his mother was saying as she stood up. "And it'll probably never happen at all. The man'll come and say that's the only rotten board in the house, I'll sell fifty acres of riverfront Monday morning—"

"Mur, all we have to do is find the Money Room, and we can fix up a dozen houses!" Lindy said earnestly.

Her mother looked down at her a moment, smiling a little. Then she said gently but very decidedly, "Yes, but I'm laying down a new law, effective *now*. No more searching! The old house can't take it, and neither can I. You could easily have broken a leg, not just a board." She opened a drawer, handed Lindy the glue and some old rags, and pointed Scotty toward the broom closet where the vacuum lived. "Now go on up and start working on that mess."

"I don't *want* that old Dorrie Suggs to buy our house," Lindy muttered as they lugged their equipment up the stairs. "I don't want to move, either." She gave Scotty a glance, half-reproachful, half-questioning. "I s'pose you'd rather go back to Medford."

"No," he said. "Not really." That wasn't the problem either, he discovered. The fact was, he had no more desire to move back to Fortieth Street, or the apartment or Gramma Holloway's house, or even some altogether new place in Medford, than he had to move to Cedarvale. And now he thought of it, he wouldn't want to move back to Cherry Street either—not now, not without Dad.

Then what do I mean, *Back home in Medford*? he asked himself irritably. And all at once he knew. He meant—not just

Cherry Street, not just the room with the tartan wallpaper and Donnie McBee next door, but that other whole life, that other time, before his father died, when the days ran along under cloudless skies and your parents held up the world. He wanted to move back to *that*.

And it couldn't be done. Not now, not ever.

He reached the top of the stairs and stood there, feeling the knowledge sink into him like tiny particles of lead, filtering into every cranny, every limb, weighting him to the floor.

"Well?" Lindy prodded. "Then what do you want?"

He shrugged his heavy-feeling shoulders. "I'd rather stay here. Let Mur have what *she* wants for a change." If she can manage to hang onto it, added a strange new doubtful voice in his mind.

"Okay. Then we've got to keep on searching, somehow or other—never mind her new law. We'll just have to find some other *way* to search."

Scotty nodded, collected the pythonlike coils of the vacuum's hose, and plodded after her into her room.

CHAPTER VIII

Mur did not sell fifty acres of riverfront on Monday—but Scotty did get an answer to his letter to Gramma Scott in Washington, D.C., which he had finally got around to writing on that rainy Sunday a couple of weeks before.

Unfortunately her reply was slightly scatterbrained, like Gramma Scott herself, containing a great many exclamation points and no information at all about the Money Room.

"You know Scotty honey I was only an in-law!! not a *real* Scott, and never really knew your grandad's father very well . . . or his mother either, come to that!! I was a Baltimore girl—I met your grandad here in Washington when he came to work in the Library of Congress. We always *wanted* to travel West to see his parents, but it's a long way!! And oh, my, during the Depression nobody had two dimes to rub together!!! Of course your mama used to visit the Oregon folks a lot—she just fell in love with that farm at first sight and had *no* use for the East Coast ever after. But your great-grandfather always paid her fare for those trips, he just loved having her come. He used to say she was Scott clear through, just like her dad, and I guess he was right, I never could see much sign of my Baltimore side of the family in her. Well, Scott honey, I'm afraid I can't tell you much but it's all so long ago. How are you and Melinda? How is school? My, I wish I could see you both!!! . . ." And so on.

"She calls me Melinda," said Lindy in a rather pleased voice.

"Well, that's your name," Scotty reminded her, putting the letter back in the envelope.

"Yeah, but nobody ever calls me that. I forgot she did. I wish she could see us, too. D'you think we'd ever go to Washington, D.C. again? Don't answer that question." Lindy went back to her Monday afternoon job of cage-cleaning, at which she was working with the smooth, stately movements of a duchess, chin up, neck straight, so as not to dislodge Binkie, who was resting cozily on the shiny top of her head.

"You know, that could be good for your posture," remarked Scotty interestedly. "Like those African ladies who carry jars and things on their heads."

"African ladies?" Without relaxing her regal pose, Lindy turned to give him a puzzled stare. "Listen, Scotty, do you think *you* could get used to calling me Melinda? I wish somebody would. You know, if I'd thought of it, I could've told everybody at this school that was my name. Darn! A perfect chance to start fresh, and I missed it. Binkie, can you say 'Melinda?' Say Melinda! Melinda!"

"Dirty bird," said Binkie comfortably, in his strange little ventriloquist's burble.

"Yes, you're a nice little dirty bird," Lindy assured him.

"I don't know why I thought Gramma Scott could help us anyhow," Scotty mused. "Somebody who'd always lived around *here* would be a better person to ask. Maybe the oldest person in Dover." He tossed the letter on top of the rest of the circulars and bills he'd just brought in from the mailbox. "I wonder who the oldest person in Dover would be?"

"Anybody but old Snerky Suggs," said Lindy balefully.

"I'll ask the postmaster," Scotty decided as he collected his books and headed upstairs to do his homework. "I'll drop by the post office tomorrow, right after school."

The postmaster, Mr. Kidder, was only middle-aged himself, but as Scotty had guessed, he knew everybody and had lived in Dover all his life—his mother having been a Wrenowski. He was interested at once in Scotty's question, seemed flattered to be appealed to, and took off his glasses to think about it.

"Well, sonny, let me see now. Oldest person around. There's my wife's pa, of course. He's eighty-two. But he only moved out here with us couple of years ago. You want somebody *native*, right? Hmm. There's Dorrie Suggs—but I think old Frank Schubert's a good bit older'n Dorrie. Only thing is, old Frank's not as bright as he once was, and you wanted to *talk* to 'em, right? Some kinda interview for school, is it? Now you just gimme a minute, I'll think of somebody, you come to the right person . . . I got it! Old Mrs. Vickery. Ruby Vickery, Box 102, comes in here for her mail ever' day of the world. She's up in her eighties somewhere, I'd stake my gold collar button on that. You go see her. Lives all by herself, edge o' town—you know that gravel lane leadin' toward the Colby road?"

"Oh, sure! That runs right past the foot of our orchard."

"That's the one! Okay, well you go on along that lane a piece and you'll see the house—little house with white shutters. Can't miss it!"

"But—" Scotty was beginning to have qualms. "How should I—maybe I could take her mail to her, as a sort of excuse?"

"Can't let you do that, sonny, without her say-so," Mr. Kidder told him. "Tell you what, take her this advertising newspaper. Only junk mail anyhow. You just go right up and knock on 'er door. She likes visitin'. Used to be good friends with Cora Elmer, and *that* one could talk your arm off. Be sure you speak up, Ruby's a little harda hearing."

"Oh, I will. Thanks a lot!" Scotty took the newspaper and hurried out to his bike, rejoicing at his luck. A good friend of Mrs. Elmer's—as well as the oldest person around! She might have known Great-Gramp.

He knew Great-Gramp a good deal better than he had before the Great Search on Saturday. The thin little leather-bound notebook, with which he had spent an absorbed hour Sunday, had left him with a remarkably clear impression of the old man's personality, almost of his voice. The diary was only two-thirds filled, the first entry dated in November, 1931, shortly after Great-Gramp's retreat to the farm. Obviously he had started it for something to do while he convalesced, though he apparently took little interest in it—perhaps in anything, at that point. The early entries were brief and factual: "Rain again today. Pretty steady for a week now." "Elmer tells me no money in the prunes these days—wants to pull down a few of the trees and plant apples." "Chimney caught fire last night. Had the sweeps in today from Cedarvale, cleaned the thing.

Hadn't been touched in years." "Christmas. Not up to much celebration, nor can't think of much to celebrate. Kate gave me a good warm throw for my knees. Need it, sitting around all day like an old has-been. Not going to use it though and look like one."

He didn't even mention finances or the loss of his business and fortune until well into January. "Big ad in the Portland paper today—that fellow Ferris who bought the store, he's going to open next week with a big sale. Pictures of lamps, underwear, clothes, curtains, shoes—looks like junk to me. Glad it won't be Scott's Emporium any more, with that kind of stock."

There were a few entries that made an odd shiver run down Scott's back, as if he had suddenly touched a living bit of history. There was one for March 1st, 1932: "Terrible thing. Somebody's kidnapped Colonel Lindbergh's baby." And another, undated, "General Motors selling for $7\frac{5}{8}$ today. Radio for $2\frac{1}{2}$. Way down from where I sold out last summer. I'm having the newspaper stopped. Just gives me the dismals, and I'm trying to forget all that."

By mid-April he was beginning to succeed in doing so: "I told Elmer he could pull out those prune trees. No profit in apples, though—spuds, either—waste of time and land. Heard of a fellow down the valley a ways, doing pretty fair with filbert-nuts. Got a hunch he's onto something." Later that month: "Played a hunch and bought a hundred baby chicks for Cora Elmer. Not sure she was best pleased. Woman can't stop talking long enough to do a simple sum." And on the first of May: "Walked all around the property today. Nice day, nice walk. Not too tired, either."

From then on the entries became infrequent and finally stopped, crowded out as Great-Gramp got busy creating his prosperous filbert and chicken business out of that one-horse farm. Now *there* was somebody, Scotty reflected, who knew all about starting over.

There was one entry that stuck especially in Scotty's mind, and he was puzzling over it again as he turned off the lane into a footpath leading toward a small, white-shuttered cottage. It was one of the last entries in early June: "Heard Max McEwan died yesterday—came on the radio. Doubt if I've set eyes on him since him and me went broke together in that shoe store, back in 1911. Couple of crazy kids, didn't know what we were doing, gives me the fantods to think how we kept those books of ours. But we had a mighty good year or two. I've probably had more good years than most folks. Best ones behind me now, but in a manner of speaking, I've still *got* 'em. One way of looking at it, anyhow."

What had he meant? Scotty hadn't understood that when he read it, and he didn't understand it now. How could you still *have* years that were all past and behind you? Gone and finished and vanished and no more to be brought back than Dad could be brought back from his grave?

"Well, mercy on us! What a nice surprise! Did you ride clear down here a-purpose to bring my newspaper?"

Scotty came to with a start to find himself standing in front of the open cottage door, in which stood a beaming, dumpling-shaped old lady leaning on a cane—the same he had bumbled into one day in the post office.

"Oh. I—yes, ma'am, I did, Mrs. Vickery. I'm Scott Holloway, and Mr. Kidder said—"

"You'll have to speak a little louder, pet, I don't hear like I used to. Come in, come in outa that wind. My, the breeze has got up, hasn't it? That'll bring the nuts down! Seems like I've seen you someplace before. Live around here, do you?"

"Yes, over there. Where Mrs. Elmer used to live," Scotty pointed as accurately as he could while being ushered hospitably into a tiny living room, which at first glance seemed to be entirely full of outsized tulips on bright blue chintz—on the draperies, lampshades, two fat chairs and a fatter sofa, on a multitude of little ruffled cushions heaped on the window seat.

"Oh, yes," Mrs. Vickery said vaguely, smiling and nodding but not, Scott suspected, having much idea of what he had said, though he had obediently raised his voice. He was glad to see she was leading him right through the tulipy room into another, furnished much less strenuously and more comfortably as a sort of sitting room with a kitchen at one end. "I was just about to fix me a cup of cocoa," she went on. "You like cocoa, don't you? Now let me just find where I put that old hearing aid. . . ."

She began rummaging in drawers and peering into little china boxes and ornaments, of which there were a great number standing about on tables and whatnots and shelves and the sills of a row of sunny windows overlooking the lane. Scotty had just begun to take all this in what he was startled by an odd, cackly voice saying, "Good morning, George!" in just the way the old lady might have said it if somebody had been strangling her as she spoke. Scotty wheeled around, his hair lifting slightly, saw her still burrowing in a drawer. Wheeling the other way, he finally noticed the tall, hooplike stand near the windows, and a chubby gray parrot with a scarlet tail hanging upside down from the top of the hoop, craning its neck to stare at him with a calculating yellow eye. "Morning, George!" it repeated.

"Oh. Hi," Scotty murmured, resisting the impulse to mention that his name wasn't George. He was still staring at the bird, who seemed perfectly comfortable upside down, when Mrs. Vickery hobbled toward him, one hand adjusting something at her right ear. "There now! Nuisancy old thing—I don't like it, but I've got to have it, and there's no use pretending I don't. I see you've met George. Bid good-day to the young man, George!—though I suppose he already has. Now, then, tell me about yourself. Did you say something about Cora Elmer?"

"Only that I live where she used to. We—"

"Oh! Then you'll be the Thatcher boy. Now that's funny, I thought that boy was a bit smaller'n you." She gave him a puzzled scrutiny as she measured cocoa into a pan.

Hastily Scotty explained that he was not Barney Thatcher, but Scott Holloway, and that he hadn't meant *that* house, but the *other* one Mrs. Elmer had lived in, and—

"Oh, the old Scott Place! Of *course!*" exclaimed Mrs. Vickery as she turned with delight to look him over again. "You'll be little Janet Scott's boy. Now, I've just been *wanting* to get a look at you—used to know your mama when she was no bigger'n a minute. And your own name's Scott?"

"Scotty, most people call me."

"Of course they do. That's what they called your great-grampa, too—just 'Scotty.' Scotty," she repeated with a little sigh, smiling as she heaped a plate with fat sugar cookies.

The parrot suddenly joined the conversation. "Shoot the moon, Scotty! Thousand aces and double pinochle! Thousand aces and double pinochle! Shoot the moon, Scotty! Awrrrrrrk!"

Scotty whirled toward the big oval perch, as Mrs. Vickery broke into a peal of laughter. "Oh, will you listen! He caught that name!"

"Did *he* know my Great-Gramp too?" Scotty asked her.

"Mercy yes, as well as I did. Knows how to play a hand of pinochle too, I shouldn't wonder—he was always right there in the room with 'em while they had their game. You want the striped mug or the big blue one? Let's sit down and be cozy. You carry the cookies."

Wishing you could ask a parrot questions and expect to get answers, Scotty accepted mug and cookie plate, and followed her to her faded easy chair. Folding himself rather awkwardly onto the low ottoman next to it, Scotty sipped his cocoa and ventured, "Did Great-Gramp play pinochle here?"

"No, no, this house was my sister's then. I lived out t'other side of Dover, on the old Suggs place. That's when I was keeping house for Dorrie Suggs and his youngest boy Joe. Runs the feed store now—he was still in grade school when his ma died. They fixed me up a room—used to be the woodshed—and I did for 'em. Always had George in the kitchen with me, same as now, and they always played those Tuesday night pinochle games on the kitchen table. Your great-grampa and old Doc Martin—he's long gone too—and a couple of the younger men, Frank Schubert and Dorrie. And—"

"Double pinochle, Dorrie!" squawked the parrot. He followed this with a loud, chortling laugh and added, "In the Money Room, Dorrie, where else? It's in the Money Room!"

Electrified, Scotty slowly unfolded from the ottoman, staring at the bird. "What is he saying? What does he mean? Does he know something about the Money Room? Do *you*?"

CHAPTER IX

When Scotty started homeward nearly an hour later, he was full of cookies and the sense of having made friends with a delightful old lady, but he knew very little more about the Money Room than when he came—except that it had been Great-Gramp's favorite sport to tease Dorrie Suggs with it.

"Oh, he was a great one for a joke, your great-grandpa," Mrs. Vickery had told him, laughing first at her memories, then—till the tears stood in her eyes—at George, who, once started, went right on practicing his Money-Room speech at a deafening yell for five solid minutes. When he subsided at last, distracted by Mrs. Vickery's offer of a slice of apple, Scotty begged to be told what the bird was talking about.

"Was there really a Money Room, or was it just a joke?" he asked. "Mur—my mom thinks it was just some old family joke. But there must've been *something* behind it—don't you think so?"

"Mercy, child, I don't know. I heard about it, a-course. My

lands, we all did—at one time the rumors used to run around Dover like they was on wheels. But I never reckoned there was any actual *treasure* room. I'm a sensible woman. And for sure your great-grandpa was a sensible man—not one to stuff his money in a mattress or somewheres and then go along and crow to the world about his Money Room! Goodness! Seems to me he'd been more likely to buy livestock—or more farmland. But I do know one thing—he enjoyed a joke! Land alive, I've seen him sit there and lead Dorrie on about somethin'—straight face, y'know, never crack a smile—"

"And Dorrie—I mean Mr. Suggs—believed it?" put in Scotty, enchanted.

"Oh, Dorrie'd believe anything," Mrs. Vickery said with a flap of her hand, then instantly reversed herself. "Well, I don't mean *that*. Be mighty hard to fool Dorrie if it was something to do with buying and selling farmland—or driving a close bargain. That man'll go halfway 'round Robin Hood's barn to fix some deal the way he wants it. Oh, Dorrie's shrewd, always has been. Greedy, too. No, all I mean is, he'd believe most anything your *great-granpa* told him."

"But—why?" asked Scotty.

Mrs. Vickery thought a moment. "Well, honey, your great-granpa was an older man, and such a different sort of man from him. Different as eggs from bananas, and Dorrie knew that. Goodness! Been to France and Spain and I don't know where-all and had that fine, big department store up in Portland—his own store, with his own name on it, Scott's Emporium, known all over the state. And—oh, all that other kind of life he had before he came here. Big money, big world that Dorrie didn't know beans about, just *wished* he did." She glanced at Scotty, her faded blue eyes amused and tolerant. "He was just kinda bedazzled, Dorrie was. And in my opinion, honey, he never knew when your great-granpa was joking him and when not. That's just my opinion, but I've heard 'em at it, many and many a Tuesday evening, over those pinochle games! And so has George!"

"Hello, George!" screeched the parrot. "Double pinochle, Doc, double pinochle! A thousand aces!"

"Oh, you and your thousand aces," said Mrs. Vickery placidly.

"So you think Great-Gramp just invented the Money Room on purpose to kid Mr. Suggs?" Scotty persisted.

"Oh, well, no, not on purpose, he wouldn'ta done that, pet, your great-granpa was a kindhearted man for all his crusty ways. It pro'ly came up sort of by accident, just a passing remark. I don't know. But he never teased Dorrie just to be mean. It was more like he was trying to get Dorrie to *see* he was joking. But Dorrie never did. Oh, he pretended to, and he'd laugh, but you could tell he wasn't real sure which was true and which wasn't. And that was what tickled your great-granpa. My land alive, he'd *laugh*—! At himself, too—he made a-many a mock of himself, and of human nature. He didn't hold any high opinion of human nature."

"But what'd he *say* about the Money Room? What was it supposed to be?"

"Goodness, what he *didn't* say!" Mrs. Vickery chuckled and shook her head, making that little clucking sound that only old-fashioned old ladies make—a sound George immediately echoed with virtuoso skill. "I declare you never heard such foolishness. Doorknobs plated with gold, fifty-dollar bills stuffing the pillows, piles of boxes sitting around the place, all full of silver soup spoons—well, I don't know what all! You wouldn't have thought *anybody*'d believe it."

"But Mr. Suggs did?" Scotty couldn't help giggling, while at the same time feeling just a *little* sorry for old Dorrie, sitting bedazzled, swallowing all Great-Gramp's tall tales.

"Well, Dorrie's kind of a dreamer, in a funny sorta way. He likes to dream about money. A-course he knew your great-granpa was exaggerating. But he thought there was a fair-sized molehill under the mountain, all the same. And maybe there was, maybe there was, but not the kind he was dreaming of, I'll bet my buttonhook."

"What did *you* think the Money Room was, Mrs. Vickery?"

"Why, I thought it was just your great-granpa's private office. The one he used to have in the big store, maybe—or even the one he'd set up at home here in Dover, for his farm accounts and all. I know he had one right there in your house somewheres—he mentioned it more'n once."

"I wonder where?" Scotty mused. "I know. There's a little sort of sun porch off the living room, with bookshelves, and a desk. My mother calls it the Nook."

"Now, that might be the very place. How *is* your mother?" Mrs. Vickery passed the cookies once more and settled back cozily. "Tell me all about yourself!"

To his own surprise, Scotty found himself doing so. Mrs. Vickery was easier to talk to than anybody he'd ever met. Since George soon elbowed his raucous way into the conversation, they did a lot of laughing together, too. She was a mine of funny information on the ways of parrots. When he reluctantly took his leave, it was with a firm invitation to come back, any day, or every day if he chose, and the feeling that he'd made an odd but interesting friend.

He lost no time in telling Mur and Lindy about it as they all circulated around the kitchen that evening performing their predinner chores. "So that's how come nobody ever knew anything but rumors," Scotty finished as he set Gretel's dish on the porch for her. "Or else thought it was just an old joke. Because it was Great-Gramp started the rumors and made the jokes! All to see how much he could get old Dorrie to swallow."

"You mean this Mrs. Vickery doesn't think there even *is* a Money Room?" demanded Lindy.

"She doesn't know. I don't either. But I'll bet old Dorrie still thinks there is—and *that's* why he keeps trying to buy our house!"

"Oh, Scotty!" Mur laughed and scooped the mashed potatoes into a bowl. "That's really stretching things, isn't it?"

"Have you got a better theory?" Scotty challenged.

"Well—a more realistic one. I think old Dorrie has a developer on the string and thinks our property might land him. I wouldn't be a bit surprised if he had options on Joneses' and Chaverses' already—everything else this side of the road."

Lindy gaped at her, outraged, holding a captured but still protesting Binkie. "They'd put condominiums all over Fred's pasture? And the holly orchard? And the creek? But they'll *spoil* everything!"

"Tell me about it," Mur said ironically. She heaved a big sigh, set the platter of chicken on the table, and dropped into her seat. "Whooo! What a day. Come on, I'm famished."

"What was the matter with your day? Was it yicky?"

Lindy popped Binkie into his cage and slid in on the other side.

"Very yicky. Would you believe I have three listings where I have to do something complicated about *cats* whenever I show the house? Scotty, get the butter before you sit down."

"About *cats*?" echoed Lindy.

"Cats. At one house I'm not supposed to let 'em in, and at the others I'm not supposed to let 'em out! And they lie *in wait* for me to open a door. I spent a good half the morning chasing one or the other of them."

"Did you sell any of the houses?" Scotty asked her.

She grinned wearily. "If I had, I wouldn't be complaining about the cats. Oh, lord, there goes the phone again. Never mind, Scott, it'll be for me. I just hope it isn't Mr. Mayberry."

"Is he the one with all the children who needs five bedrooms and a real big loan?" Lindy asked Scotty as Mur answered the call.

"No, he's the one who keeps raising the price on his falling-down duplex," Scotty told her. Their mother's clients were faceless but familiar characters to them both.

But it was not a client phoning this time. Mur came back looking upset and began to eat in preoccupied silence.

"Who was it?" Scotty asked uneasily.

Mur buttered a roll and then sat holding it as if she'd forgotten what it was for. "It was Henry Baxter's daughter. You know, the picking-machine man. She says Henry's back 'went out on him' today. I gather it's not the first time."

"Oh. Does that mean he's sick, or just—"

"It means he's in the hospital, in traction." Mur dropped the roll back onto her plate. "Now what? He was planning to start on Wrenowski's orchard the first of the week and pick here next."

Scotty and Lindy exchanged an uncertain glance. "Oh, well," Scotty said. "Our nuts still aren't all down yet."

"They will be soon, with this east wind."

"Maybe by then he'll be okay. Or—couldn't *we* just pick them? Scotty and me, and Carol Jane, and—"

"All nineteen tons?" said Mur.

"Nineteen *tons?*" Scotty echoed incredulously.

"That's what Henry's estimating—at least a ton to the acre."

It seemed more nuts than there were in the world. Even Lindy was silenced—but only momentarily.

"How long does he have to stay in traction?" she demanded.

"They don't know yet. Maybe only a day or two. I *hope.*"

"Well, anyhow, there's bound to be other people with picking machines. Can't we get somebody else to do it?"

"I don't know. I suspect they're all booked solid by now."

"But—" Lindy stared at her in dismay. "But what'll we *do* if Henry can't pick our orchard?"

"Lindy, I just got the phone call! At the moment, I don't *know.*"

It was a lot of things *not* to know—about something they'd thought was all settled. But as Mur said, there wasn't much they could do till they heard from Henry's doctor and found out where they were.

Meanwhile the sun shone and the east wind went on blowing, polishing the sky, making biking a chore, and bringing the filberts rattling down in the orchard. Scotty took Mrs.

Vickery at her word and dropped by to see her again Wednesday afternoon; on Thursday, with her ready permission, Mr. Kidder let him pick up her mail.

"This is a real favor to me, pet," she told him earnestly as she led the way through the tulipy chintz into her kitchen. "A little walk's good for me in the ordinary way, but I can't *abide* east wind! Gets my sinuses acting up. George, say hello like a nice bird!"

"Shoot the moon!" yelled the parrot.

"Oh, *tsk, tsk, tsk*," said Mrs. Vickery. "Have you time to sit down, Scotty? I made apple brownies this morning. Tell me if you've had any word about Henry Baxter! I declare, that *back* of his! What's your mama going to do if he doesn't get all right?"

Scotty could only say, "I don't know." He accepted a brownie, but since it was nearly five o'clock he left very soon, promising to come back Friday, when school would close early for a teachers' meeting. A few minutes later, pedaling against the buffeting wind around the curve into the driveway, he spotted Carol Jane's dandelion-fluff head—always a beacon against the dark green Oregon backgrounds—as she stood with Lindy beside the laurel hedge at the back walk. Both of them were looking toward the orchard. He swung off his bike and joined them, automatically turning to look too, though there wasn't much to see from here except tossing branches.

"So what happens if they just can't be picked when they're s'posed to?" Lindy was asking.

Carol Jane shrugged. "Well, it starts to rain, along about Hallowe'en, or sooner. Then the picking machines can't get in."

"Well, but sooner or later it *quits* raining. The ground would dry off again."

"Not enough. Not once it really starts in bein' rainy. Even when you can walk around okay yourself, the machines bog down, and there y'are. And by Christmas those nuts'll soak up so much water wouldn't be any good to you anyhow. Cost too much to dry 'em."

"But—but then what *happens* to them?"

"They just lie and rot."

Oh, come on, thought Scotty, suddenly rebelling against this picture of unrelieved gloom. "Has that ever really happened?" he challenged.

"Yep," said Carol Jane. She rested her solemn, pale blue eyes on him a moment. Then she turned away. "I gotta go home and feed the pig."

Scotty and Lindy trailed silently into the house.

At least the wind stopped blowing, sometime during the night, and Scotty rode to school Friday through a soft, shifting fog that made the pumpkins in Schuberts' roadside patch glow like lopsided wintry suns. By the time he left Mrs. Vickery's that afternoon, after a fine unhurried hour enlivened by some of George's saltiest comments, the orchards stood still and silent as collections of glass trees, not a leaf stirring, not a nut rustling down—as if they were *trying* to wait for Henry.

Thanks to the teachers' meeting and early dismissal, Scotty reached home about three-thirty in spite of his visit to Mrs. Vickery—half an hour before he'd normally be getting out of school. And tomorrow was Saturday, too, he reflected with a pleasant sense of leisure. Nobody else was home yet; Lindy, he knew, had gone to Cedarvale with Carol Jane and her mother, and of course Mur's schedule was unchanged. But Gretel had no holiday plans, as far as he knew, and unaccountably, she too was missing from her post on the screened porch.

It seemed odd. Scott walked through the downstairs, calling her, then went out the front door and northwards around the house. He had no sooner rounded the northwest corner than he saw the ladder—a heavy old homemade ladder he'd often noticed lying in the weeds out beside the barn. Now it was lying smash across the camellia bush under the Nook's west windows—the bush Mur had said was her favorite—squashing it out of recognition. Wincing at what she would say to those broken branches, Scotty was hurrying to drag the ladder off when the strangeness of its being there at all made him stop and stare. The freshly broken twigs, the position of the ladder, as if dropped in haste—the whole scene had the look of something that had only just happened. For the first time, Scotty's gaze moved from the unfortunate bush to what lay directly above—the low, almost flat roof of the Nook jutting out from the side of the house, and slightly to the right above that, but not much above, the dormer window in Lindy's room.

Then had Lindy done this somehow? Before she left for Cedarvale maybe? Scotty couldn't believe it. The ladder—obviously Mr. Elmer's handiwork of an earlier day—was homemade of a couple of fourteen-foot two-by-fours with scraps of board nailed across for rungs. Even with Carol Jane to help her, Lindy could never have got that thing from the barn to here. Scotty wasn't sure he could handle it himself, without further damage to the bush. Anyhow, why would Lindy want it here? He could imagine no reason. But if some intruder had been prowling around—maybe a tall guy with red hair—then why hadn't Gretel gone into one of her watch-dog tantrums?

Of course, maybe she *had*. Where *was* Gretel?

Abandoning the whole problem of the ladder, Scotty yelled "*Gretel!*" and took off at a run down the north side of the house, around the outside of the adjoining back fence, and through the gate into the yard. His eyes went anxiously to the pump house, but there was no little vigilant sausage-shaped figure posted at the hole under the side wall—nor anywhere else around the little building, as Scotty discovered by circling it. Even as he was telling himself not to panic, that Gretel could just as well be staring, deaf and dumb, at some other hole somewhere else, he heard odd, unidentifiable bump-ing noises coming from *inside* the pump house. They were only slight sounds—erratic and rather stealthy, as if somebody were quietly doing something. But what would anybody be doing? In a pump house?

Holy Maloney! thought Scotty, going all over prickles. Damaging the *pump*?

Forgetting caution, he leaped for the door handle and yanked—thus discovering that the door was latched, by one of the ubiquitous wooden tabs set high up on the outside. He fumbled this aside, realizing he'd never even known it was there, and yanked again, this time hurling the door wide open.

And there was Gretel, prone on the cement floor beside the pump platform, busy with a bone that would have challenged a St. Bernard. At Scotty's uncouth entrance she glanced up, thumped her tail in a preoccupied way, then readjusted a front paw over the bone and began again to create the erratic little sounds he had heard.

He backed out of the pump house and stood a moment on the walk, feeling as if his brain had got stuck in neutral. It seemed extraordinarily hard even to get from A to B, much less make sense of this jumble of peculiar happenings.

Somebody had given Gretel a bone, he reasoned laboriously. Somebody had let her out of the porch and *then* given her the bone—in the pump house—and then locked her in with it. *Why?*

To keep her out of the way while he set up the ladder, answered the voice of logic.

But who was "he"? There wasn't any tall red-haired guy, really. And even the grinning Chaverses would scarcely go dropping huge ladders onto Mur's favorite camellia bush. Maybe . . . Mur had said something about asking Walt Thatcher, who was Barney Thatcher's father, to patch up that broken place in the. . . .

And then he thought he had it. The dry-rot inspection. Probably Mur had asked somebody to come—he *had* come— nobody home—Gretel wouldn't let him in. . . .

Scotty was suddenly on his way to the potato cellar. While he could not feel he had fitted together all the puzzle pieces— for instance, what dry-rot inspector would just happen to bring along an enormous bone, and why had he left the ladder there?—it had occurred to him that if Lindy had been here awhile between arriving from school and departing to Cedarvale, she might know all about it, in which case she would unfailingly have left him a coded message to explain.

He covered the stretch of fog-dampened, weedy ground

at his briskest trot, bounded down the short flight of cement steps, and pushed the old door open. He stepped confidently in—and felt an explosion of pain on the top of his head. Bells clanged, lights flashed, and the floor came up to hit him.

CHAPTER X

It was raining—sort of in handfuls—on his face only, which was odd. And a high, rather husky voice was querulously going on and on about something, from just above his left ear. Among other things it kept telling him to wake up, though he *was* awake, and more than ready to get up, because this bed was hard as a rock, and—

Scotty stirred, and his head gave a great throb. After a paralyzed instant, memory rushed back. He opened his eyes just in time to receive another handful of water in them. Sputtering, he dragged his sleeve across his face and sat up.

"Well, that's progress," said the fretful voice. "Do you want to drink some of this or anything? I rinsed out the can."

Scotty found himself gulping cold water tasting faintly of fresh-ground coffee, and blinking up into the worried, freckled face of Barney Thatcher, who was holding the coffee can to his lips, still complaining. "I *told* you to watch out for that guy! How come you didn't pay any mind?"

Scotty pushed away the can. "Oh, w'zat you?" he said thickly. "W'zat him? Tall red-headed? Ladder?"

"Sure it was. C'mere, I'll show you. Can you stand up?"

Scotty got somewhat shakily to his feet, one hand to his head, and teetered after Barney out the door and up two of the cement steps. Peering cautiously toward the barn from behind a screen of weeds, he caught a glimpse of a lanky furtive figure with an unmistakable fiery thatch, just departing hurriedly for the road. Not a man. A boy, possibly high school age.

"He put the ladder back," Barney explained. "I warned you about him! I knew he'd come snooping around again! I *told* you!"

"Well, I don't know what you thought I could do about it," Scotty protested, turning back toward the cellar. Then, realizing there was no need to go there now, he faced Barney instead. "Who is he, anyhow? You find out?"

"Not exactly. But my pop says there's some kind of nephew of old Dorrie Suggs, from over at Colby, that's got red hair."

Dorrie Suggs. I might have known, Scotty thought. Still staring into Barney's freckle-sprinkled face with its light-lashed, blue-green eyes, he suddenly realized this was *Barney*, the standoffish Thatcher boy who didn't want to know him, who avoided him at school and on egg-days, who. . . . *Barney* had written them that warning about the red-haired guy? "How come you never answered our note?" he demanded.

"What note?"

So they went back into the cellar after all. Scotty reached for the drawer, then remembered. "Oh. I tore it up. It was there nearly a week," he added accusingly.

"Well, how'd I know? I only looked in those drawers once or twice." Abruptly, Barney's face went bright red, and he half turned away, giving his usual impression of retreating behind the sheepdog fringe. "My pop says you'll think I hang around here all the time—trying to butt into your business. But I *don't*. I haven't set foot in here since the night . . . since I left that message about the red-haired guy."

"Since the night the firecracker went off!" Scotty stared. "*You* set off that firecracker?"

"Yeah." Barney's eyes slid around to meet his, wary but with a gleam of laughter in them.

"To scare that guy off?"

"Yeah. It worked, too. He shot outa here—"

"My sister *said* she saw somebody! We thought . . . where was he, anyhow?"

"He was down here, in the cellar. Hiding. He'd been snooping around the whole place, but your ma came home from work, so he ducked in here—prob'ly meant to wait for dark. Well . . . *I* was snooping around too." A half-defiant, half-defensive glance. "But not to butt in where I wasn't wanted. Only to find out what *he* was up to. 'Cause I'd seen him on this property before, and I knew he hadn't oughta be. When the Elmers lived in your house I used to kind of . . . watch out for no-goods. They liked me to. I didn't mean any harm, or—"

"Listen, *we* don't mind. We'd've helped, if we'd only known it was you, that night. Where were you when he ducked down here?"

"Up in the shed," Barney said triumphantly, waving to

the ceiling, which of course was the shed's floor. "And look here." He beckoned Scotty to a far corner, pointed up to a jagged knothole that took a sizable bite from the edge of one of the old floorboards. "That's where I dropped the firecracker through. Just put a match to 'er and let 'er go."

His face split in a grin of unadulterated glee, which Scotty felt his own face mirroring. "Wow. I wish I'd seen him."

"It was great," said Barney simply.

"Then what about today?"

"Well, today he showed up a lot earlier, but 'course he didn't know about that teachers' meeting—prob'ly figured nobody'd come home till he was gone. I was delivering the Wrenowskis' eggs, is how come I happened to spot his car—he had it parked up the road there, in a turnoff. So I sneaked back here along the edge of the creek, and I saw him just climbing down that ladder from the little roof that sticks out there—that low one—"

"The Nook roof. Was he looking in windows or what? Lindy's window's right above there."

"There's *three* windows right above that roof—two dormers and a regular one. He could've just walked right across and peeked in all of 'em, for all I know."

True, thought Scotty, visualizing the north side of the house. Three windows—Lindy's dormer, the bathroom window, and the dormer beside his own bed.

"But by the time I got here he was halfway down the ladder," Barney said regretfully. "So I dunno what he'd been doing. He was standing dead still, listening—prob'ly just heard you come home. Next minute he jumped off the ladder—started trying to lug it outa the flower bed, but then just dropped the thing and lit out for *here*—practically straight at me. But I dived around behind the shed, and thank the lord he made for the cellar. He couldn't get away because *you* kept walking around in plain sight. What were you doing?"

"Hunting for Gretel. Our dog. He'd locked her in the pump house with a big bone. When he first came, I guess."

"Didn't want her to bark," said Barney. "Well, anyhow, you kind of had him pinned down, and he had *me* pinned down, so then when you charged out here all at once like one of us had *called* you and straight in that door without even—well, he clobbered you with a hunk of wood. And took off. Did he hurt you very bad?"

"I don't think so." Scotty put a cautious hand to the top of his head. It was excruciatingly tender but no longer throbbed unless he moved suddenly. "He was probably trying not to. Hey. By the way—thanks for . . . you know, the water and all." Abruptly he felt self-conscious again.

"Oh. Wasn't anything. Creek was right there handy." Barney scowled toward the cupboard, looking as uncomfortable as Scotty felt. Why do we keep *doing* this? Scotty thought, exasperated. Like a couple of strange dogs trying to decide whether to fight or get along.

Barney said suddenly, "What'd the note say, anyhow? The one I never found."

"Oh—it just said, if you're a friend, tell us who you are. Something like that."

The blue-green eyes swiveled toward him, wide with surprise. "Who'd you *think* I was, an enemy? When I was trying to *warn* you?"

"Well—I suppose you'll think it's dumb," Scotty said

stiffly. "But I thought it was those Chavers guys. Pulling another trick on us. They *did* pull one. Sent me and Lindy both way down to that big stump, each of us thinking the other. . . ." Scott halted, watching Barney's face go fiery again. "*You* wrote those phoney notes that day!"

"Yeah."

For a moment Scotty stared at him. No gleam of mischief in Barney's eyes now; he looked embarrassed and miserable. "But *why?* If you wanted to be friends."

"Just one of my lousy ideas." Barney gave a small twitch of a shrug and looked resignedly at Scott. "My pop says I'm a real flop at making friends. I do all the wrong things."

"I'm not much good at it either," Scotty mumbled. All at once he could clearly see how—at the over-enthusiastic moment—those duplicate notes might have struck Barney as a hilarious idea, bound to make all three of them boon companions. It was the sort of boner he'd often pulled himself, until he'd learned to avoid all boners by making no overtures whatever. Of course, that way you avoided making friends, too. "Lindy and I should've caught on that it was a joke. But we—I guess we were just dumb. Anyway, you live so much farther away than the Chaverses—"

"No I don't. Not if you take the short cut." Barney turned to point. "From the creek straight through the back corner of the fir grove. It's real close. I'll show you tomorrow." He scanned Scotty's face anxiously. "If you want me to."

"Sure, I do. I always did want to sort of—get acquainted. But then Gretel started right off biting you, and anyhow . . . well, I thought you weren't interested in making friends. You always kept clear of me at school."

Barney's jaw sagged. "I thought *you* kept clear of me! Fact is, I thought you were kind of stuck-up."

"Everybody always thinks so. I guess I act stuck-up," Scotty said helplessly.

A rueful glimmer showed in the blue-green eyes. "Well, *I* act like I'm not interested in friends."

Their smiles, tentative at first, spread into a couple of sheepish grins.

"Wanta go in the house?" Scotty said. "I don't know what we're standing around out here for anyway; I'm starving." As they set off across the rough ground, he added, "The thing is, I figured you probably knew everybody in school already."

"I don't know hardly anybody." The little twitch of a shrug again. "We've only lived here five years. And they stick together at that school!"

"I know," Scotty said with feeling.

"Even on the bus. That's how come I ride my bike."

"Me too. Hey, we might ride 'em together. Every day after school I go exploring places, and we could—"

"Nope, I gotta tear right home after school, or my pop'd have my hide offa me." Barney grinned with pride at this ferocity, and listed a few of his after-school duties: gather the eggs, water the chickens, dig the spuds for dinner, climb back on his bike to make that day's egg-deliveries. "My pop does the morning chores, though. We could ride *to* school together. That is—" He paused, then added awkwardly, "Would your sister be along?"

"She takes the bus." Puzzled by the abrupt change in his tone, Scotty turned to find him scarlet and apologetic.

"Your sister doesn't like me," he explained, glum-faced.

"*Lindy?* But she likes everyb—" Scotty stopped. "Well, maybe she got a sort of wrong impression right at first, because of Gretel. But wait'll she finds out you were the friend warning us about the red-haired guy! She *said* there was an unknown friend. That's why I left that note."

"Oh." Barney's expression lightened a little. After a moment he went on, "Listen, how come that red-haired kid keeps turning up here, anyhow? What's he *want?* And what's more, I saw old Dorrie Suggs walking all around this place one day. *Him*—old man Elmer wouldn't let 'im on the property! They had some kinda feud."

"I'll bet I know which day you saw him," Scotty said, remembering the Monday of the flailing, and Mur saying she didn't know how long old Dorrie had been there when she came home. "I think they're both looking for the same thing. Old Suggs probably gets this nephew kid to come spying so *he* won't get caught doing it himself. Sounds just like him."

"But what're they doing?"

Scotty hesitated. *What if he thinks I'm stupid? What if he laughs at me?* At the screen door he turned to watch Barney's face, then plunged. "Lindy and I think they're trying to find the Money Room. Some folks believe there's a lot of money hidden somewhere on this place."

The reaction was all he could have asked for. Barney's mouth dropped open, his eyes widened until the thick light lashes looked like the rays from blue-green suns, and his very freckles seemed to dance with curiosity. "*Honest?* How come they think that? Whose money is it? Why'd they hide it? Have you guys been hunting for it? Can I help you?"

Scotty felt suddenly home free, warm and dry. He laughed and pulled open the screen door with a gesture of blissful abandon. It banged and bucked against the house, only partially satisfying the exhilarated thing inside him that wanted to leap and caper and grin like a Hallowe'en jack-o-lantern. He knew exactly how Lindy had felt on discovering Carol Jane. "Come on in!" he urged Barney. "I'll tell you all about it!"

During the half hour or so before Lindy got home, Barney found out as much about the Money Room as she knew. Barney and Scotty also found out a lot about each other, but not nearly enough, and Scotty had the happy sensation that the two of them could go on talking for ages without running out of things to say. They'd already discovered they had a remarkable number of things in common, ranging from a taste for peanut-butter-and-pickle sandwiches to having only one parent. Barney's mother was still living, but not even his pop knew where, and Barney went so stiff-faced and inarticulate at the mention of her that Scotty hastily dropped the subject, abruptly aware that there might be something even more painful than having a parent die.

Barney was much more forthcoming about "my pop," who was plainly the fixed star around which his life orbited and final authority on almost everything, as well as top boss of his many labors in garden and chicken house. These were unpaid and—Scotty gathered—largely unthanked, but Barney seemed to regard numerous chores as a fact of life and the absence of a chewing-out as praise enough. Scotty got a picture—reinforced by a glimpse or two he'd had of Walt

Thatcher—of a silent, heavy-shouldered man, always busy, always working, seldom smiling. Remembering his own dad, he could only reflect that it took all kinds.

Somewhere around four-thirty Lindy erupted into the kitchen, overflowing with news about the Cedarvale shopping mall and Carol Jane's new boots, but the sight of Barney stopped her in mid-spate. "Oh. Hello," she said forbiddingly.

"Listen, Lindy," Scotty began, but already Barney, fiery-faced behind his sheepdog bangs, was scrambling up from behind the curve of the breakfast table muttering, "H'lo, Melinda." With an I-told-you-so glance at Scotty he added, "G'bye, I better go," and would have gone, despite Scotty's protests, had not Lindy said in an entirely different tone of voice, "He called me 'Melinda'!"

Barney paused, shot her a wary glance and said, "Isn't that your name?"

"Yes, but nobody hardly even knows it. Everybody mostly calls me Lindy."

Barney jerked his head at Scotty. "*He* said your name was Melinda—that first morning I brought the eggs. But I'll call you Lindy if you want," he added hurriedly.

"No, I don't want! I *like* to be called Melinda." All suspicions forgotten, Lindy beamed at him as if he had done something extremely clever—which he had whether he knew it or not, thought Scotty as he struggled not to grin. Then she glanced at Scotty, and her beam changed to a puzzled stare. "Why does your hair look so funny?" she demanded.

"My hair?" Equally puzzled, Scotty reached for his head and winced. "Oh. Because it's got a big goose egg under it. I got conked on the noggin."

"Conked?" Lindy's mouth fell open; all the suspicions were back in her glare at Barney.

"No, no, *he* didn't conk me—he saved me!" Scotty told her. "Sit down. You've got a lot to hear."

By the time she had heard it, reacted at the top of her voice, and asked a good many more excited qustions than anybody could answer, her approval of Barney was unmixed and his self-consciousness had all but vanished.

"But the cast-iron *nerve* of it!" she repeated in perhaps her third variation of this remark. "Looking right in my *window!* What do you s'pose he thought he was going to see?"

"Same thing you thought *you* were going to see when we first moved here—something that looked like a Money Room," Scotty told her.

"I did not think that! I was looking for something secret, and hidden—I never s'posed you could see it through a window!" Lindy gave a scornful wave toward the back window and broke off in mid-gesture. "Hey. Where's Binkie?"

Scotty's head, then Barney's, swiveled toward Binkie's open cage.

"Oh-oh," said Scotty. "When did you let him out?"

"Right after school!" Lindy cried. "Why didn't *you* put him in again?" She leveled an accusing finger at him. "I told you! *This morning* I told you—that I was going to Cedarvale and I'd let him out before I left and when you came would you please catch him and put him in, and you said—"

"Holy Maloney, I forgot!" Scotty was already on his feet, heading guiltily for the stairs. "You look down here, I'll go up. Wow, that's three hours he's been loose—hope he hasn't binked anything important. Stick around, Barney, we'll be right back."

But a moment later he forgot Barney, forgot to feel guilty, forgot the sore lump on his head, as he thrust his head into his own room to sweep an impatient glance around and suddenly focused on the wall beyond his two east windows. For a stunned instant he simply stood and gaped. Then he let out a yell that out-decibeled Lindy and brought the other two pounding up the stairs to his side.

Mutely he pointed to the southeast corner of his room, where Binkie, clinging to the edge of a window curtain, was still busily at work. Above and beside him for a space nearly the size of a sheet of newspaper, the wall was no longer covered with roses, except in strips and ribbons and patches that had resisted his energetic beak. Instead, it was covered with green and white rectangles of varying sizes, fitted edge to edge in that latticework pattern Scotty had so often noticed in the early morning light.

"Stocksenbonds!" gasped Lindy. "Scotty! They're Great-Gramp's stocksenbonds!"

"Bound to be—they're just like the ones in the attic!" Scotty was as breathless as she. He gave her a look of mingled excitement and hilarity. "How d'you like that! Binkie's found the Money Room—and *this* is it!"

CHAPTER XI

❖

"You mean—that's money?" said Barney in a voice that sounded as if he were completely hollow inside.

Scotty, who was feeling much the same way, said, "As good as. Or they were once. Holy Maloney—d'you suppose they're all over the whole wall? The whole room?"

All three of them advanced as one on the area of Binkie's handiwork—or beak-work—and began enlarging it in all directions. The rose paper stripped off easily, once you got a fingernail under the edge. Obviously it had been hung by an amateur—probably Great-Gran—and the heavy paper of the certificates underneath had an almost waxy surface which had resisted paste. Everywhere they explored they found more green and white rectangles.

"But the funny thing is I thought we *looked* under all the wallpaper—that day we were hunting everywhere," cried Lindy, running to a different wall to pry loose another corner.

"I know we did! We looked in *this* room. And there were lilacs underneath."

"There still are," Scotty told her, cautiously lifting the edge of one of the certificates, where it butted up against the window frame. "We just looked too *far* under." It was easy—now—to see that the certificates were between two layers of wallpaper. "Great-Gramp must have covered up those lilacs himself. I don't blame him!" Another thought struck him. "Hey, you know what? I'll bet *this* room was his office—the one Mrs. Vickery said he had somewhere in the house. It wasn't the Nook at all."

"Are any of these things worth money now?" Barney asked in the same hollow, slightly shaky voice. He was still standing before the first certificate he had cleared, staring in a dazed manner at the words on it. "This thing says 'shares ten dollars each'—and it's for *forty shares!*"

"Well—you can't believe everything you see," Scotty said, but he found that his own voice was shaking slightly, and his hands were too. It *couldn't* be that all these once-so-valuable papers were totally worthless—not every single one! He burst out, "Maybe Great-Gramp put the good ones here—the ones he thought might get to be worth something again someday. And those few in the attic were the really dead ones. D'you think that could be? If the companies didn't actually go *clear* out of business, they might sort of recover after a lot of years, mightn't they, and—"

"Yeah!" Barney agreed. "And even if these were only worth a couple dollars a share, well goshalmighty, here's one says 'a hundred shares,' and this one's fifty, and this one is too, and—" His voice had climbed an octave and he was peeling off paper as fast as the others now.

"Here's a *two* hundred one!" exclaimed Lindy. Suddenly she whirled to face them, eyes wide behind her glasses. "Scotty, you know what? You're right! Great-Gramp put these here to save them—and then he hid them! *He* put the rose paper on top!"

"Why, sure!" Scotty breathed, staring in admiration at his brilliant sister. "Sure, he must've. That's exactly what he did!"

Mur's voice sounded plaintively from the hall. "Hey, are you deaf? I've been calling and calling and—" She appeared in the doorway and broke off with a gasp at sight of Scotty's room. "My *word*. It's the demolition squad. What on earth. . . ." She was silent, staring. "Scotty, what am I seeing? Are those—"

"They're stocksenbonds!" Lindy shrieked, bouncing up and down. "Great-Gramp's stockensbonds! It's the Money Room—I *told* you there really was a Money Room, I said all along—"

"And Great-Gramp did it, he fooled everybody!" Scotty broke in eagerly. "Especially old Dorrie Suggs on account of him believing everything Great-Gramp said, and I still think that's why he keeps poking around here and wanting to buy our house—and this afternoon Barney saw *another* guy here, a big kid, spying, and . . . oh, this is Barney Thatcher, Mur . . . what's the matter?"

Mur was looking at him oddly—her face had changed at first mention of old Dorrie. But she only shook her head and turned to smile at Barney, who went bright red and smiled ecstatically back.

"And this other guy is old Dorrie's nephew! We think he was trying to spot the Money Room too, and—listen, d'you remember that night we thought there was a gunshot? Well. . . ." Scotty hurried on, aided by a good many interruptions from Lindy and even a few from Barney. He glossed hastily over his personal encounter with the nephew in the potato cellar, but filled Mur in on the rest, while she leaned in the doorway listening, and looking around the disaster area in front of her with a very complicated expression on her face. "So there was Great-Gramp," he finished, "kidding old Dorrie about gold-plated doorknobs and making all those jokes, and all the time—"

"And all the time," Mur said with a little one-sided smile, "he was aiming the joke at himself."

The others gaped at her. "At himself?" Lindy echoed.

"Of course. It sounds just like him. Securities all turned into worthless paper—so, all right, paper the walls with them! It's exactly the sort of thing he'd do. But he'd never hide it, Lindy—his whole point would be to leave it in plain sight, to make its comment. *His* comment—on fools and their money. On human nature, including *him*."

"Oh," said Scotty, rapidly descending from Never-Never Land to arrive with a jar in the ordinary world. Mrs. Vickery, too, had said Great-Gramp always mocked at human nature, and at himself.

"*Oh!*" Lindy wailed. "You mean they're not worth anything after all? You don't think he put the rose paper on, or—"

Mur shook her head. "Gran probably did that after Gramp moved his office down to the Nook. I supposed he didn't like to climb the stairs—it must've been long ago, when he was still recuperating, because when I used to come out here the Nook had been his office for ages. This room was the guest room, where I slept—and this rose paper was here then."

"Well, it's been here long enough!" Scotty said. "I'm *glad* we made a mess of it. Though it was Binkie started the demolition job."

"Yes, I assumed that. Well, go ahead and finish it, if you want to." Mur sighed, straightened from the doorjamb and brushed her hair off her forehead with a tired gesture. She did look awfully tired, Scotty suddenly realized, even depressed—and definitely she had something on her mind; she hadn't even noticed the goose egg he had carefully avoided mentioning in his resumé of the afternoon.

"You mean—we can go ahead and peel the rest of the roses off?" he asked her.

Mur nodded. She looked at him again in that odd way, then at Lindy—as if she had something to say that she couldn't get out. "Sure, why not?" she began. She stopped, then finished in a rush. "Let old Dorrie repaper."

At first Scotty thought he hadn't heard her right, then he knew he had, because of the awful sinking feeling he was beginning to have inside. Before he could get a word out, Lindy said scornfully, "Old Dorrie! What's *he* got to do with it?"

"Everything, I'm afraid," Mur answered. "I . . . it's become absolutely necessary—" Again she stopped. Then, baldly, came out with it: "I've sold him the farm. I had to. I did it this afternoon."

Nobody said anything. For a minute nobody even moved. Then Lindy wailed, *"Mur!* Without even *asking* us?"

Mur turned to her swiftly. "Oh, honey—I'm *sorry*. But

there wasn't time—it all happened so fast—"

As Mur's arms went around her, Lindy's disbelieving face crumpled into a mask of woe, and Scotty, unwilling to watch that, and somehow unable to look at Mur, instead looked at the half-stripped walls of the Money Room, then, with a pain in his throat, at Barney—whom he found staring owl-eyed at him in a way that was just how he felt, himself.

Binkie, forgotten by everyone, suddenly uttered one of his piercing *cheeeeeeeps!* and sailed from the curtain rod to land officiously on Lindy's head.

"Oh, go away!" she sobbed, and flapped a hand at him.

Mur put out her finger while he was in mid-flutter, and when he perched on it, captured his toes firmly with her thumb. "Come on, everybody. I want a cup of coffee," she said, and with an arm still around Lindy's shoulders, led the way downstairs.

Half an hour later the four of them were still sitting around the breakfast table. "Mur, you *can't*," Lindy was saying for the fourth or fifth time. "Not to that awful old Dorrie Suggs!"

Mur didn't bother to explain again. The situation was perfectly clear by now. Scotty knew Lindy went on protesting simply because she couldn't think of anything else to say. There wasn't anything else to say. And it was time to be feeding pets and starting dinner and making a stab at homework, and Barney kept looking at the clock, but nobody moved.

"Just after we finally found the Money Room!" Lindy mourned.

"If we'd found some money, instead, everything might have

been different," Mur said drily.

"We don't *know* they're all worthless!"

"It's a pretty sure thing, honey. Half the certificates I saw up there were Merchant's Bank and Trust shares, and I know that bank went totally bust. I noticed some Hunter and Company shares too, and that's long gone."

"We haven't got all the wallpaper off," persisted Lindy. "We *might* uncover—"

"Lindy dear, the deed is done. I've sold. You just have to live with it."

Scotty sighed and slumped against the back of the seat. He'd already made his protest—that Mur hadn't given in last time old Dorrie asked. She had merely pointed out that she hadn't then had the dry-rot inspection. This morning she'd brought a man out herself, followed him around and seen with her own eyes how much damage had been done, how much money it would take to put the old house to rights— several thousand dollars just to stop the deterioration, let alone renew the wiring, put on a new roof, jack up and brace the north corner where the foundation was crumbling. "I'd rather sell than watch the old place go to rack and ruin right before my eyes and know it was my fault," she said. And in a way, Scotty saw her point.

It didn't change the way he felt. I wouldn't care! I wouldn't *care!* something in him kept protesting. He tried not to blame her, tried hard to see it from her angle, told himself crossly that he'd probably see it her way quick enough if it were *his* old falling-down farmhouse—but in his heart he felt he'd have clung to it, brainlessly or not, until it did fall down.

Lindy was clearly feeling the same way. "Old Dorrie'll

never fix the place up," she grumbled.

"He might sell it to somebody who will," Mur said, but her tone lacked conviction. With an obvious effort she pushed on. "It isn't just the dry rot. It's all those nuts—that wind brought every last one down. And with Henry out of action, I guess permanently—"

"Permanently?" Lindy echoed.

"He'll be out of the hospital in about three weeks. But the doctor says he'll be right back in, unless he gives up farmwork altogether and takes some other job. I got that cheerful news just this morning."

Scotty swallowed, thinking of Carol Jane's equally cheerful picture of rotting nuts. "You mean our filberts'll just lie there?"

"Not only ours but Wrenowskis', and Charlie Kuhn's—a lot of us were counting on Henry. Of course, I've been on the phone for a week—I guess we all have. But it's way too late. All the contractors are signed up till kingdom come. So that's another several thousand dollars I was *sure* of—I thought—and now won't have."

Lindy muttered, "Old Dorrie won't worry about the orchard, either!"

"Probably not." Mur sighed. "All he wants is that vast profit he thinks he's going to make someday."

Barney, who had sat mute as a blown-out candle since they came downstairs, suddenly ventured a question. "Then is Henry just gonna sell his picking machine?"

"I suppose he will. His daughter said he'd probably take the job of custodian at the school. He'd already been offered it before this happened."

Barney merely nodded. After another glance at the clock

and a little restless squirming, he found a pause in the conversation, murmured, "I guess I better go home," and departed. A few minutes later Scotty, sitting slumped on his backbone while Mur silenced Lindy's last mournful protests, found a new thought stirring in his mind.

He muttered, "I'll bet it's all connected."

"What's all connected?" Lindy said crossly.

"The ladder, and the red-haired guy, and old Suggs making a new offer. It's got to be!"

Mur was looking at him blankly. "What ladder? What red-haired guy?"

"Why, you know," Scotty was beginning, when Lindy cut in.

"She *doesn't* know! We only just barely mentioned him. Mur, there's this nephew of old Dorrie's, and today he was—"

"Wait a minute!" Scotty flapped an impatient hand. "Mur, what time did old Dorrie phone you?"

"He didn't. I phoned him. About one o'clock."

"Oh. Then maybe my theory's no good. But it sure is *funny. . . .*"

"Will you tell me what you're talking about?"

So they told her—about the ladder, the red-haired nephew, the conk on the head, about what Barney had seen. About Gretel.

"Gretel!" exclaimed Lindy, startled into movement. "I'll bet she's still out there stuffing herself on that bone!"

Abruptly she left to find out; just as abruptly Mur pulled Scotty over to examine his goose egg in the brighter light over the sink.

"It's okay, he didn't hit me very hard," Scotty protested,

trying to squirm free. "It doesn't even hurt much unless I touch it."

"I'll have the law on him anyway," Mur said through her teeth. She peered ferociously at the lump a moment longer, parting Scotty's hair with her fingers and exploring the area all about it before admitting with obvious reluctance that it didn't actually seem serious. Scotty got the impression that she'd have loved to find a drop of blood, so she could leap into the car that instant, hunt down the big red-haired boy wherever he might be, and bash *him* over the head repeatedly —maybe old Suggs, too.

"The point is," he went on as she finally turned away to reach under the sink for potatoes, "why d'you suppose that guy was prowling around our house, trying to peek in windows?"

"A very good question—one I'm going to ask the sheriff," she told him grimly.

Scotty, who had thought the question merely rhetorical, stared at her. "But it's plain as day old Suggs sent him to find the Money Room—probably paid him to snoop. And listen, I got thinking about that roof. It goes clear across there, over the Nook. He might have been peeking in *my* dormer window, not Lindy's. And if he did, he'd have seen what Binkie was doing—he'd have seen the stocks and bonds!"

Mur's hands had paused, a potato in one, peeler in the other, as she leaned on the sink to laugh—a bit hysterically. "Oh, Scotty! And then presumably dashed for his car to go report to Uncle Dorrie! My, you and Lindy die hard!"

"Well, if *you've* got a better—"

"Now, wait, don't get your back up. It's a neat theory—

but it just won't work! I phoned old Dorrie the minute I got back to the office after that dry-rot inspection—before I could change my mind! And that was before Binkie was even out of his cage."

"Yeah. Well, in that case I don't know why he wants the place."

"I've told you why."

Scotty heaved a sigh. "Okay. But you might've got more money if you hadn't phoned him so fast. Because once he got that word from his nephew—Why, he might've doubled his offer!"

"Not that old horse trader." There was no amusement in Mur's voice now. "In fact, I thought he'd lost interest. I wasn't a bit sure, when I phoned. . . . But he had the whole deal primed to go. He'd ordered the title search made *three weeks* ago, got the contract drawn up all ready to finish. The minute I said yes, he took off for Oregon City, told his lawyer what terms to fill in, rushed over to his bank. First thing I knew he was back in my office plunking down a cashier's check for the down payment, and saying, 'Sign here.' We wound the whole thing up in less than two hours." She looked as if she still felt a little dazed. "The man's like a bull-dozer. I got everything I asked for, though." She tossed a potato into the pan and added with a slightly defensive air, "What's more, I made him give me earnest money to cover that two hours he was gone. Fifteen hundred dollars. Made me feel a little better."

Half to himself, Scotty said, "I still think it's the Money Room he's after. And Holy Maloney, once he sees those stocks and bonds—"

"Scott, don't torture yourself, he's not going to be gloating over your wallpaper. Heavens, he went through the Great Depression himself! He's a lot too sharp to think those things are worth any fortune—whatever we think of his personal charm."

"Which I'd hate to tell you what I think of it," said Lindy scornfully, reappearing at that moment accompanied by Gretel, who waddled straight to her basket and subsided, presumably to sleep off her Gargantuan meal.

"But Mur, Mrs. Vickery told me—"

"Scott, I *know* what Mrs. Vickery told you. Here, be useful." Mur captured Scott's hands, put the salad bowl in one and a head of lettuce in the other. "Lindy, set the table. And let's give this subject a rest."

No more was said. At the time, there didn't seem anything left to say.

We've lost the war, that's all, Scotty thought as he went gloomily upstairs after dinner. It's over. Just as so much was *beginning.*

Before turning on a light, he wandered across his room to the tall east windows and knelt there, elbows on the sill and chin on his fists, staring out into the lavender dusk. He'd never wanted to come to Dover in the first place. Now here he was, all broken up at the thought of leaving. He'd never have believed, two months ago, how much he would hate giving up this farm—how much he had found here. Not only the fir grove and the Place of the Arrowhead, and the workshop in the barn that he'd barely got to use yet, but this old house with all its reminders of Great-Gramp—almost a crusty old ghost-in-residence—and the trees full of apples, and the countryside that he knew like the back of his hand by now, and the postmaster and Mrs. Vickery and George—and Barney. He was even going to like his room, without those roses. Or would like it, if it could only be his.

But it couldn't be his now. It was old Dorrie's. Because of Mur. *Mur* had lost the war for them all. She'd just—surrendered.

He hated thinking that; it made him feel as if each foot weighed five hundred pounds. He tumbled it out of his mind before it had a chance to settle. And to keep from thinking instead about some stupid new house in Cedarvale and a stupid new room and new school, Scotty got up and turned on the light and began peeling more roses off the wall.

CHAPTER XII

◈

Scotty woke up to a Saturday as dreary in prospect as Friday had been attractive. Just to live through it seemed a burden. At breakfast even Lindy was listless, and shortly afterwards headed gloomily for Carol Jane's to break the news. And Mur, who had arranged for a morning off for housecleaning, got a phone call from her client with all the children and had to drop everything and go to Cedarvale, to show him another big house he'd spotted.

"He won't be able to pay for that one either," she told Scotty as she found her purse and the car keys. "I think I'm going to have to find him an abandoned office building or something." She glanced at Scotty, who didn't meet her eye. "Why don't you get Barney to come over?"

But Barney wouldn't be free of chores until after lunch.

Scotty stood by the kitchen window and watched the station wagon start for Cedarvale, then limply kept on standing there as the now-familiar Saturday morning traffic went back and forth on the road that used to seem so empty—first Herman Evans with his cow, then Sam Wrenowski's pickup going the other way, then the lady with the old Chevy who worked in the Dover drugstore, then two of the Chavers boys on one bike, with their big curly-tailed dog panting along behind. . . . Those Chaverses hadn't done anything mean after all, he'd just thought they had. They might not be so bad once you got to know them. . . . A truckload of somebody's filberts went by—safely picked and headed for the drying-plant—then old Mr. Schubert on his tractor with the big disk attached, rumbling and clanking along about two miles an hour, with four cars trailing close behind because the disk took up most of the road. The third car was the mail carrier's jeep, which pulled up by the mailbox and shook Scotty out of his stupor. Nearly ten o'clock!

He roused himself, went out for the mail, then up to his room, where he spent an hour peeling the rest of the rose paper off the walls. After he'd swept up the scraps, he stood a moment wistfully admiring Great-Gramp's effect. It looked simply great, that irregular pattern of green and white rectangles—almost better than Stewart tartan, and a huge improvement on roses. And talk about unusual! *Nobody* had a room like this one; maybe nobody ever would again.

A few minutes later he wandered out doors, and down along the side of the filbert orchard. The orchard floor, weed-free and smooth since the flailing, with each tree trunk rising from a pool of dark shade, no longer looked clean and bare under low-drooping branches. Now it was cluttered with shiny brown nuts; they lay in swathes, in thick-layered circles, thinning to a random sprinkling in the sun-dappled alleys between rows—and the limbs, relieved of their weight, sprang high.

A ton to the acre. Destined to lie there and rot.

Quickly Scotty ducked under the fringe of wild rose vines, hoping for some comfort in the Place of the Arrowhead. But when he climbed over the barrier log and stood again in the little mossy room with its ferns and water music, he could think only that he was going to lose it along with everything else. He sat down on Chief Mucklechuk's moss-cushioned throne and stared around him, trying to memorize it all. He had never had a place so totally his own, so special—though he'd never intended to keep it that way forever; he'd meant to show Lindy sometime. It wasn't her kind of place, but she'd like it, and she wouldn't encroach. It *was* Barney's kind of place, Scotty suspected. He wondered: would he bring Barney here? Share it with him? There were ways in which it would be even better, shared with just the right person. If he were going to stay—

Maybe I'll leave it to him as a sort of present, he thought, standing up and jamming his hands into his pockets. Tell him how to find it after I'm gone.

He walked back to the house and took his current library book out under the Gravenstein tree, where he slouched morosely in an ancient yard chair the rest of the morning, turning pages.

When he came in for lunch, Mur and Lindy were both in his room, admiring his wallpaper. Moodily he joined them.

"A little eccentric, but then your Great-Gramp never was like anyone else." Mur gave a laugh—slightly forced, Scotty thought. She was peering hard at some of the certificates, a slight frown puckering her dark eyebrows, bending double sideways to read the ones with words going up and down, squatting to see those near the floor.

He said rebelliously, "Seems hard to believe they could *all* be worthless."

Mur straightened. "Well, I'll bet my second-best diamond earrings they are. However. I have to admit I don't really *know* about some of them—quite a few."

Scotty's heart gave a thump, and Lindy stopped admiring the decor in a hurry. "Mur! D'you mean it's *possible* there's some good ones?"

"Just *barely* possible. Not probable. Not probable at all."

"But aren't we going to find out?"

It was a while before Mur answered. She sat down thoughtfully in Scotty's desk chair and finally looked up at them. "Do we want to? They belong to old Dorrie now."

"I don't see why!" Lindy said hotly. Her glasses assumed a scheming glint. "Listen, Mur, couldn't we just—"

"No, we could not just peel them off the wall," Mur told her firmly. "When a person sells a house, he sells everything physically attached to it—that's the law. And it goes double for real estate agents. We can't take our unusual wallpaper with us." She stood up. "It'll turn out there's no reason to. But I suppose I ought to check up. I'll call my boss. He's got a stockbroker in his family somewhere—his sister's husband, is it? Maybe his wife's sister's husband. In either case—"

The rest was lost as she headed for the phone downstairs, Lindy clattering at her heels. Scotty dropped into the desk chair himself and took a long, bothered look around his room

—old Dorrie's room. Half of him was wishing hard the stocks would turn out after all to have *some* value, the other half feeling he couldn't bear it if they did. It was a while before he could decide for sure that he hoped the stocks were worthless—since they were old Dorrie's now. Then he followed the others downstairs. By that time Mur was on the phone to somebody—a stranger, Scotty could tell by her voice.

"Well, I must say that's extremely obliging of you," she was telling whoever-it-was in that astonished, appreciative way that always made people eager to do something else for her instantly. "Yes, you'll find it a beautiful drive out here, this time of year. . . . Well, all right, we'll look for you. I'll have the coffeepot on." Mur hung up and turned, the astonished, appreciative look all over her face as well as in her voice. "What an awfully nice man!"

"The boss's wife's sister's husband?" Scotty hazarded.

"The wife's sister's husband's *father*, as it turns out. James D. Berrington—*the* Berrington of Ames, Berrington, Stokely and Ford—very impressive! It's a big brokerage firm in Portland." Mur grinned suddenly. "He said he grew up in a family where P.R. Scott was a household word and Scott's Emporium something to swear by, like the Bible, and that he wouldn't miss that Money Room for the world. He's coming out tomorrow afternoon!"

Lindy's face abruptly sagged. "*Tomorrow?*"

"Listen, my girl, I thought we'd do well to get somebody by the end of next week—if ever!"

"But it seems such ages—what'll we *do* with ourselves till then?"

Scotty, who was feeling the same way but hadn't been going to say so, flashed a cautious glance at Mur. To his surprise, she didn't just tell them to go clean their rooms or something.

"I know what we'll do with the rest of today. We'll go to Cedarvale and look at houses."

That was worse than cleaning their rooms. "You did that all morning!" Scotty protested.

"Don't I know it! But one I saw this morning might do for us." Mur's glance moved from one to the other of them. "Don't go closing your faces on me. Or your minds, either, please. Our house is sold. We have to find another. The only way to do it is to look. Now come on, let's rustle up a peanut-butter sandwich or something, and then we'll go."

They went. Glumly, they looked—not just at one house but at four. They were nice-enough houses. The one Mur had thought might do was only a block from the school and within walking distance of her office. It had windowseats with storage in two of the bedrooms, and lots of bookshelves, and fresh paint and no dry rot. The neighbors were rather too close on each side, but that had never mattered in Medford. Riding back to Dover in the silent car at the end of the afternoon, Scotty realized he would have liked that house fine if he had never lived on Great-Gramp's farm, never known what it was to have ranging space and woods and a barn and a whole shabby, spacious, beckoning kingdom of his own.

He stole a glance at the two profiles beside him in the front seat—both closed and expressionless. Nobody had said a word since they left Cedarvale. He suspected the others were feeling just as he was himself.

Lindy proved it by saying in a small voice, "If it only

hadn't happened so *fast*. We hardly even got to live in Great-Gramp's house yet. I'm not *ready* to move."

Like a dam giving way, Mur burst out, "Oh, Lindy, I know it happened fast! I keep asking myself whether I just let that old operator rush me into it when my resistance was down. . . . But it's done. I can't get out of it now." A moment later, in a flat, no-nonsense voice, she added, "It's still the sensible thing to do, remember. Nothing has changed, the problems haven't gone away. We'll live."

A few minutes later they turned into the rutted, gravelly driveway. As they rolled along beside the dusty rhododendrons toward the screened back porch, they saw Barney Thatcher stand up from the big stone that held the garage door open, and cup both hands around his mouth to shout something in the direction of the filbert orchard. Then he hurried over to open the car door for Mur, looking anxious but eager.

"Hello, Mrs. Holloway, my pop wants to tell you something. Ask you something," he said in his husky, high voice. "If it's okay? Hi, Scotty. Hi, Melinda."

The Holloways said "Hi," and Lindy's face of woe even relaxed somewhat as she turned to regard him kindly. Scotty added, "What's up?" but Barney only mumbled something incoherent—his attention was all on his father, who had appeared through the fringe of shrubs that screened the orchard and was crossing the humpy grass toward Mur with his heavy countryman's tread.

Mur said, "Hello, Walt," and put out her hand.

Mr. Thatcher took it briefly, unsmiling, nodded his greeting. Not a man to waste words, Scotty reflected. Or energy in being polite. Still, he wasn't being impolite—just coming straight to the point, saying Barney'd told him she was worried about the filberts.

Mur said, "More than worried. I'd contracted with Henry Baxter, but—"

"I talked to Henry this morning. I'm taking over his jobs."

Mur's eyes widened. "You're going to harvest all those orchards for him? Ours, too?"

"Do yours first, if you like. It's ready." Mr. Thatcher paused, glanced down at his shoes, then faced her squarely again. "Boy says you've sold the place."

"Yes, I couldn't see any way out. I didn't want to, but—"

"Sorry to hear it. Harvest is yours, though. He can't claim that."

Nobody needed to ask who "he" was. Mur said, "No, but I never thought I could get it picked. This is a real break, believe me! How are you going to . . . I mean, have you got a—"

"I'll use Henry's machine, pay him part of my take." Mr. Thatcher sounded almost as if he'd been hoping for the question. There was an odd hint of excitement in his voice. Suddenly he blurted, "Going to buy that picking machine from Henry. He gimme an option." For an instant his eyes sparkled, his whole face came to life, as if a curtain had lifted to reveal an entirely different man. Just as abruptly, the curtain fell again as he added impassively, "That's if I can get a loan."

Scotty, glancing at Barney, saw the glow reflected like a sunset, shining and magnified in every freckle. Pulling him aside as Mur and Mr. Thatcher went on talking, Scotty asked, in some awe, if that was why he had slipped away yesterday, to tell his father about the picking machine being for sale.

"Yeah! My pop's been wanting a chance to get one of those things secondhand ever since we moved here! I ran all the way to Ed Schubert's place to tell him. He quit work right away and went to phone Henry's sister. Got in first with his offer." Barney's grin was blinding. "He said it was his lucky day."

Scotty returned the grin, not without difficulty, remembering Mur's flat voice saying, *We'll live.* "That's great. I'm glad it was lucky for somebody," he said.

And that was Saturday.

About two on Sunday afternoon, the boss's wife's sister's husband's father, the impressive James T. Berrington of Ames, Berrington, Stokely and Ford, Securities, rattled into the gravelly driveway in a very unimpressive Volkswagen almost as old as Scotty, and unfolded himself like some miraculously expanding jackknife from behind the wheel. He was tall, thin, slightly stooped, with sparse, sleek hair and bright black eyes —altogether strongly reminiscent of an amiable stork as he advanced on his long, sticklike legs, beaming from Scotty to Lindy.

"Hello, Mr. Berrington," Scotty murmured, getting up from the back steps to accept the clasp of a large, firm hand.

"Good afternoon! Good afternoon!" The hand released Scotty's to sweep a comprehensive gesture around the property. "So this is old Napoleon Scott's Second Empire!" said Mr. Berrington in a cheerful, rather rusty-sounding voice that seemed to match the rest of him. "And you two are his heirs, I take it? And the reception committee!"

Scotty admitted it with a grin, rather wishing he'd waited in the house with at least a slight show of cool, but Lindy said immediately, "Yeah! We've been watching for you ever since lunch! What took you so long?"

"Lindy!" growled her brother, but Mr. Berrington merely looked apologetic.

"A bad guess as to your lunch hour," he told her frankly. "I assure you I have been champing at the bit since breakfast, Miss—Lindy, is it?"

"You can call me Melinda," Lindy told him with the sort of smile she seldom bestowed on anything less than a really special animal. "C'mon, I'll show you the Money Room!"

"After you meet our mother," Scotty amended hastily, then with a last futile snatch after the proprieties, "Excuse us for taking you in the back way."

"Oh, he doesn't care!" scoffed Lindy, who was already hauling Mr. Berrington by the hand through the sagging door and across the cluttered screened porch like a small tugboat with an ocean liner in town. "Mur! Hey, *Mur!* Oh, there you are. Here's Mr. Berrington. C'mon, let's go upstairs!"

To Scotty's relief, Mur managed to arrest Lindy's steam-roller tactics long enough to greet their storklike guest and re-establish the family claim to some sort of civilized manners. But the guest himself seemed eager to get on with the day's business, tactfully declining Mur's offer of a cup of coffee.

"Later I'd like nothing better, Mrs. Holloway. But I *must* see that Money Room before I'm quite eaten up with curiosity. You have no idea how my imagination has been working over-night. Visions of General Motors and U.S. Steel dance through my head—far juicier than sugarplums, believe me!"

Mur laughed, and led the way at once to the stairway, but warned Mr. Berrington he had better get the sugarplums out of his head. "To tell the truth, if there's anything on that wall worth more than wallpaper I'll be dumbfounded!"

And a few minutes later, after Mr. Berrington, looking taller than ever, had stood in the middle of Scotty's room, revolving slowly, exclaiming, and absorbing the full glory of Great-Gramp's sardonic joke on himself, he agreed with her conclusions. "I can scratch most of these companies on sight," he said regretfully. "There are a few I never heard of—I suspect for the very good reason that they were defunct before I ever got into the business. Still, I'll find out for sure."

He produced a small leather-bound notebook from a pocket and began listing, in meticulous, minute handwriting, all the stocks of which he was uncertain. While he was doing it, Mur went downstairs to put the coffeepot on. Scotty began helping him by doing the squatting, neck-twisting, and chair-climbing necessary to decipher names of companies and numbers of shares on the least accessible certificates, and Lindy, after staring into space a moment, left the room. Just as Scotty was jumping off his desk and Mr. Berrington closing the notebook, she came back, carrying the red tin box from the attic.

"Oh, Holy Maloney, Lindy! He doesn't want to see all that funny-money," Scotty told her.

"Why not? Anyhow, there's certificates in here, too, just like the rest!"

"But they're no good! That is—" Scotty turned to Mr. Berrington as Lindy began rummaging in the box. "We don't actually know they're no good. But my idea was that Great-Gramp put the best ones on the wall, the ones he thought might be worth something someday—and just tossed the left overs into that box." He paused, struck by another possibility. "Of course, he *might* have done it just the other way around."

"Saved out the hopeful ones and papered the wall with the junk?" said Mr. Berrington. He took the sheaf of certificates Lindy was holding out to him, leafed through them with his long, thin hands. "Well, let's see now—that one's a dead duck —that one too—Amalgamated Freight, I think so but I'd better look it up—International Fertilizer, hmm—Cascade Pulp and Paper Company, don't know. . . . CS&W Railroad, *kaput*, Northwest Bank and Trust, *kaput*, and this one's a goner, and this one, and that's the lot." Mr. Berrington handed back all but three of the certificates, produced his pen and notebook again. "I'll track these down along with the others. Now. What else have you got there, Miss Melinda?"

But by then Mur was summoning him downstairs for coffee and a piece of the lemon cake she'd made in his honor that morning, so Lindy brought the tin box of money and the piggy bank downstairs too, ignoring Scotty's whispered protests that she'd only bore the man. As it turned out, he was no more bored by the "funny-money" than the Holloways were by his reminiscences of growing up in the twenties, when "the War" meant World War I, and these very marks were piling up in Germany in a runaway inflation, and the name of R.P. Scott—he assured them—was well known all over Oregon even to small boys. Mur's face relaxed with enjoyment as she listened to him. As for the piggy bank, he was unexpectedly interested and asked Lindy if he might take it home and let his nephew go through the coins.

"He's a penny collector," explained Mr. Berrington. "And he knows a lot of other coin buffs. He might very well find some desirable items in here, especially if they're in reasonably good shape."

"Oh, they're in great shape!" Lindy assured him earnestly. "Scotty and I fished every single coin out of there one day, so I've seen 'em all!"

"Well, I'll take good care of your Great-Gramp's pig and give you a report as soon as Jim's had a look at these." He stood up, holding out his hand to Mur. "And I'll give you a report tomorrow—if I can restrain myself from going straight down to the office today, to hunt up some of these long-lost corporations. Thank you for the cake, the coffee, the company —" He offered his hand to Scotty with a grin. "And the chance to see that tough old humorist's Money Room."

In another five minutes he had folded himself back into his battered Volkswagen and bumped away down the drive.

Just as the Holloways were sitting down to dinner that evening the phone rang. Scotty answered and immediately recognized the precise, slightly rusty voice. Mr. Berrington sounded in high good humor.

"I couldn't restrain myself," he told Scotty. "I went down to the office. And I have some pretty interesting news."

"You have? Shall I get Mur? D-d'you mean"—Scotty was beginning to stutter—"d'you mean those things on my wall— old Dorrie's wall—oh, gosh almighty—"

"No," Mr. Berrington cut in firmly and quickly, and Scotty's lungs, which were feeling like suddenly blown-up balloons, began a cautious deflation. "There's not a thing on those walls worth more than wallpaper, just as your mother suspected. But one of the securities from that red tin box is something else again. Do you remember a certificate for two hundred shares of Cascade Pulp and Paper?"

"Yes, s-sort of," quavered Scotty, holding his breath again.

"Well, that company went bankrupt in the early thirties." Mr. Berrington's tone was that of a social studies teacher who really enjoyed his work. "Stock that had been worth twenty dollars a share a few years before went begging at ten cents, in 1932. No buyers. Finally in '34 or '35 another company, a big one—Northwest Paper Mills, which I'm quite sure you've heard of—took Cascade over and reorganized it, kept it afloat. After World War II it began to make money. Anybody who still had Cascade shares could get thirty dollars for them by then. By *now*—are you holding onto something, Scotty?— Northwest Paper Stock is selling for forty-seven dollars."

"And—we have—two hundred. . . ." began Scotty faintly.

"You have two hundred shares of *Cascade*," the precise voice corrected him. "Which would now equal *seven hundred and twenty-eight* shares of Northwest Paper—there've been stock splits and I don't know what all since World War II. And seven hundred twenty-eight shares at forty-seven dollars per share works out to thirty-four thousand, two hundred and sixteen dollars."

Scotty said nothing. He felt as if he were about to burst.

"Besides which," said Mr. Berrington triumphantly, "my nephew will pay Miss Melinda a hundred and forty dollars for seven of her coins."

CHAPTER XIII

◈

The Holloways did eat dinner that evening, because, as Mur said later, there were the clean dishes in the drainer to prove it. But none of them ever remembered what they ate. They couldn't help remembering a lot of what they said, though, because they kept saying the same things over and over, sounding, as Scotty remarked at one point, like a lot of cracked records.

Lindy couldn't get over her part in their sudden windfall. "If I hadn't brought that tin box from the attic," she kept marveling. "If I hadn't *insisted*—practically over Scotty's dead body—"

"Oh, come on!" Scotty would protest, then Mur would put on *her* cracked record.

"I wish your Great-Gramp could know about it! Thumbing his nose at bad luck, that's what he was doing, then after all these years to have the last laugh, surprise us with a handsome bequest—Oh, he'd have loved it!"

"There's only one trouble—I'd rather have his Money Room than his bequest," Scotty would always point out here, and then Lindy would unfailingly add that they *could* have had *both*, if only—

Then came a string of if-onlys. If only everything had happened a little sooner—if only Binkie had done his binking Thursday instead of Friday—if only Scotty had peeled back the right layer of wallpaper two weeks ago on the day of the Great House Search—if only Lindy hadn't put her foot through the dry rot and caused Mur to get the inspector—if only the inspector hadn't been able to come—if only Henry Baxter's back hadn't 'gone out on him'—

"And if only I hadn't panicked," Mur would say in a tone that instantly gave Scotty that awful sense of heaviness, of burden, as if he were wearing a stone necktie and stone shoes. "Of course, I never dreamed we'd *close* the deal that day. But then," she'd add bitterly, "I'd never done business with old wheeler-dealer Dorrie."

"Yeah, it was *his* fault! If he hadn't had everything all ready and waiting—"

"Ready to *pounce,*" Lindy would put in, smoldering.

There was a moment's silence here while they all sat and hated old Dorrie, then Scotty would finish, "So see, Mur, it wasn't your fault, it was *his.*" It seemed somehow vital to establish this. "If he hadn't stacked the cards like that you'd have had a week or two to spare, like always, and you could be telling him right now to forget the whole thing!"

And he always meant it to sound triumphant and Mur blameless, but it turned out sounding as if he'd just proved the opposite of what he'd had in mind and only made his stone shoes seem heavier and, he suspected, made Mur feel worse. She usually brought the conversation to a halt by saying briskly, "Never mind. At least we have some money, if not the farm. And that's a lot more than we expected this morning. Thirty-four thousand dollars is nothing to sneeze at."

This was true enough, and impressive enough, to produce another silence, during which they all thought about thirty-four thousand dollars. Then, sooner or later, Lindy would say, "Just think! If I hadn't brought that tin box from the attic—" And the whole thing would begin all over.

Scotty finally made his remark about the cracked records, and to turn themselves off they got up from the table and did other things. But Scotty was still plodding over the same mental ground an hour later, when he stopped on his way upstairs to do his math and said, "It's just like 'The Gift of the Magi'! I knew it was reminding me of something!"

"What's 'The Gift of the Magi'?" Lindy demanded, pausing in the act of covering Binkie's cage.

"That story—you know. It's Christmas, and this girl sells her hair to buy this guy a chain for his watch—but he's already rushed out and sold his watch to buy her a fancy comb for her hair. We read it in school."

"Nightie-night! Nightie-night!" rasped Binkie impatiently.

Lindy dropped the cover over his cage and zipped it up, saying, "What a dumb story," and adding that she couldn't imagine why anybody'd want either one of those things for Christmas anyhow.

"That's not the point!" Scotty told her. "The idea is that by the time they gave each other these fancy gifts, neither of 'em had any use for them."

"I get the point, Scott," Mur said a bit wearily. Scotty turned in dismay, his conscience giving him an exasperated clout for having made her feel bad again. But she hugged him briefly around the shoulders as she went to draw the living room curtains. "It's a bitter story. And I'm afraid things sometimes turn out just that way."

"I guess so," Scotty muttered.

But Lindy burst out rebelliously, "I don't see why we've got to hold still for it! Why don't we *do* something?"

"Just what would you suggest we do?" Mur inquired.

"*I* don't know. But I'll bet Great-Gramp would never have just sat here and let it happen!"

Scotty felt an immediate conviction that *he* should have said that. He should have thought it. He knew Great-Gramp better than anybody—at least he felt he did.

"She's right. He wouldn't! Mur? . . . Mur, could we phone old Dorrie and try to—unsell?"

Mur stood still, one hand on the drapery cord. " 'We' means me, I assume," she said drily. She stared away from them into the darkness beyond the bay window. "Lord! Back out of a deal! It's so unprofessional. . . . Of course, no more so than rushing into one the way I did. Really, this whole thing is making me look so ramshackle I'm beginning to wonder if I'm fit to be out alone—much less in charge of a family." The curtains *whoooooosh*ed across the window.

Lindy wheedled, "Oh, come on, Mur. Give it a try, okay?"

Mur drew a long breath and let it out in a gusty sigh. "All right. I got us into it, I'll try to get us out. There's a new law—something about three days' grace to change your mind, even if the deal's closed. I doubt if old Dorrie's ever heard of it. Even if he has, I'll bet my hat he'll just tell me to sue. But I'll find out."

"Right now?" Lindy asked eagerly.

"*Now?* Nine o'clock at night?" Mur looked startled, then thoughtful. "Well, come to think of it, I'd as soon not phone him from the office. All right, right now." She turned and headed for the phone, Lindy at her heels.

Scotty abandoned all thought of doing his math and followed. But he found his hopes dying almost from the first. Mur's voice, frank and straightforward as she asked for release from a decision made in too much haste under too much pressure, chilled abruptly as she added, "I beg your pardon?" She listened in stiff-backed silence to some jovial-sounding clacking from the phone—Scotty distinctly heard old Dorrie's laugh—and when she next spoke, her voice had frozen to an icicle.

"In that case, I can only hope it is never to your advantage. We'll leave it as it stands, then. . . . What? . . . No, it will not be convenient. Neither tomorrow nor any other day, until November third when you get possession—as we agreed. Goodbye."

She hung up, cutting off the last few clacks, and turned with a face as frozen as her voice.

"He won't," muttered Scotty.

"What'd he say?" Lindy demanded darkly.

Mur's expression defrosted slightly as she gave a shrug of exasperation. "He informed me—quite kindly—that bi'ness was bi'ness, and he was afraid I'd have to learn to take a few hard knocks if I meant to be a bi'nesswoman. He said even pretty little ladies couldn't go changing their minds and that anybody in Dover would tell me Dorrit Suggs never went back on a bargain, not even if it was to his own advantage."

"*Ohhhhhhh-HHHHH!*" snarled Lindy, words deserting her.

"He also remarked that he'd be wanting to drop around soon and would tomorrow morning be convenient? Well, if he sets one foot on this place before November third, I'll take him to court for trespass."

Scotty, feeling the stone necktie settle again around his collar, said, "We shouldn't have made you phone."

"It was worth a try. But that's the end of it now, Lindy."

"You didn't tell him there's a new *law*."

"No, I didn't," Mur said, facing her. "I didn't argue, either. Or appeal to his better nature. Or beg. We're stuck with this bargain. There are some things I just can't bring myself to do."

They were all silent a moment. Then Scotty, moved by a quite unexpected impulse, walked up to Mur and hugged *her* around the shoulders, patting her awkwardly as he did so. "Never mind," he said. "It'll be all right."

His hug was returned with interest; Mur's eyes—barely above the level of his own, he noticed—brightened with tears as she stepped away, went into her room, and closed the door.

Lindy watched her go, then turned to Scotty and stared. "Why'd you say that? It *won't* be all right. Will it?"

"I don't know," Scotty said confusedly. "I don't know why I said it."

"Did something make you *think* everything might—"

"No. I just—all at once knew how she felt."

"Well, me too! I mean, we all feel the same way, don't we?" Lindy eyed him a moment longer, then heaved an enormous sigh and plodded upstairs, mumbling that she might as well take a bath.

Scotty stood where he was, trying to figure himself out. They *didn't* all feel the same way—that was the point. Mur felt lots worse than anybody, because it was mostly her fault. And it wasn't going to be all right; not a thing had changed.

But oddly—now he felt a little better. The stone necktie was gone. Why? The only thing that had happened was that he'd seen Mur standing there, feeling guilty and inadequate and cornered and practically wishing she was dead—and he'd *known* so exactly how she felt that he was impelled to go and hug her. Just for one instant, *he* had felt like the parent, and she'd seemed the child.

Weird.

Slowly he followed Lindy upstairs. Mur wasn't any child. She wasn't a perfect parent either. This mess mostly *was* her fault, she *had* panicked, and she'd been outsmarted—no matter how much they all talked, they couldn't get around that. But the big difference—for him—was that he suddenly didn't care about any of that, just so she got to liking herself again.

He stood in the middle of his room and wondered if there was anything he could do about it. Before, she'd always had Dad to count on, to do something about what worried her. Now she had nobody but two kids—and he'd seldom felt more inadequate and cornered, himself.

He shucked off his clothes and put on pajamas and turned off his lamp, leaving the room illuminated only by the faint glow reflected up the stairwell. Then he sat on the edge of his bed, his eyes on the dim rectangles of the stocks and bonds, and asked himself, for the first of many times in his life: what would Great-Gramp do?

The answer came immediately: *Something bold.*

But what? How could even Great-Gramp do anything if there wasn't anything to do? How would he think something up? How would he *start?*

That seemed to be the quintessential question. Scotty combed his mind for answers, combed through everything he knew about Great-Gramp, everything he'd read in that little black leather book, searching for how one might *start* thinking up a good bold idea. All he came up with were such things as Great-Gramp deciding on filberts instead of apples and buying Cora Elmer a hundred baby chicks.

He finally stretched out and pulled the covers up, still without a coherent answer. And when he awoke next morning, the question was still in his mind.

But now the answer was there too.

How would Great-Gramp come up with one of his bold ideas?

He'd play a hunch.

CHAPTER XIV

Scotty sat straight up in bed. The sun was picking out the familiar latticework pattern on the Money Room wall, temporarily turning Great-Gramp's worthless paper back into gilt-edged securities. *Play a hunch.* That was it. That was the answer.

Planting filberts instead of apples—buying all those chicks —maybe, back in 1911, deciding to try dry goods, after that shoe store went broke . . . all hunches.

Well, I have a hunch too, Scotty thought as he swung his feet to the floor and reached for his clothes. Same old hunch I've had all along.

The trouble was . . . maybe it wasn't a very good hunch. Mur didn't believe in it . . . but Mur had been wrong sometimes. Especially lately. On the other hand, *he'd* been wrong a lot himself, not only lately but ever since he could remember. And she had all the logic on her side.

He sat with a sock in one hand and his chin in the other,

staring at the dormer window and visualizing the red-haired guy peering in here toward the patch of wall where Binkie was at work. He *must* have seen what was going on—and one glance would have been enough if you were looking for a Money Room. But why—if the hunch was any good—hadn't old Dorrie come steaming over here on Friday, as soon as he got the report? It wasn't until *Sunday*, last night when Mur phoned, that he'd asked to drop by when it was convenient.

And it wasn't going to be convenient till November third, and he apparently took that calmly too. It didn't seem a bit like old Dorrie. Wait three weeks to lay eyes on that Money Room he'd dreamed of for thirty-odd years? Maybe the red-haired guy hadn't looked in the window after all—hadn't even been on the roof. But he *had*. When Barney saw him, he was climbing back down. Or rather, just standing, about half-way down.

Scotty halted, one arm in a sleeve, staring at a sudden mental picture of a motionless figure on a ladder, halfway down.

Why not *halfway up*?

It would explain everything.

Thrusting his other arm in its sleeve, Scotty groped under the bed for his shoes. His hunch was back, stronger than ever—if only he could think what to do with it.

By the time he'd got his shoes tied, thinking furiously, he was beginning to have an answer to that one, too.

It was a long and peculiar day; up until four o'clock Scotty was only dimly aware of what went on around him, being totally absorbed with two anxious questions: before noon, whether he had the nerve to do what he meant to do at lunch break, and after noon, whether he was glad or sorry he'd done it. He later remembered only two bits vividly—first, asking Lindy at breakfast what her plans were for the afternoon and learning, with a giant thump of his heart, that she was going to Carol Jane's house for Bluebird meeting—probably her last, she added gloomily. The second vivid bit was his lunch break, which he spent pedaling hurriedly to the pay phone five blocks from school, making a call to Dorrie Suggs, then pedaling hurriedly back.

At four o'clock he put all that behind him. Too late to worry now. Before the bus had taken on its first passengers he was on his way home by the quickest route, devoutly hoping Mur would not just happen to turn up early today. Her usual hour was five.

At 4:17 he leaned his bike against the side of the screened porch and leaped for the door. Bestowing a hasty pat on Gretel, who trotted out as he strode in, he dumped his books on the table and opened the refrigerator. Three minutes later he was posted by the bay window gnawing ravenously on a carrot—he'd missed lunch to make the phone call—with his gaze riveted on the gravelled drive where it joined the road.

At 4:22, the old purplish Pontiac sedan turned in and rolled up the drive to the house.

By the time old Dorrie appeared at the back door, Scotty was there to push it open, his face arranged in an expression he hoped was civil without being exactly friendly, casual while not exactly vacant, innocent as a toddler's, just slightly blockheaded, and above all perfectly natural. The effort to sustain all this at once made him feel as though he were wearing a mask of drying cement.

Old Suggs, wearing without any effort at all his usual jovial grin, nodded genially at Scotty and sauntered past into the kitchen. "Changed her mind, did she?" he remarked as he shot proprietary glances around the room, the steel-rimmed glasses flashing. "Well, well, I had a notion she would, when she come to think it over. Can't keep a man waitin' three mortal weeks to see his own proppity! Truth is, sonny, she was just a mite put out at me last night on the phone. On'y natural. Kinda got the best of 'er in a bargain the other day, and the ladies, they don't like that. Figure we oughta treat 'em polite in a bi'ness deal, same as in a ballroom!" He tucked his big hands into his overalls bib and treated Scotty to a wide-angle view of thirty-two porcelain teeth.

"Yes sir," Scotty said neutrally. "She might still be a little put out. But she won't be home till five and you can probably see all you want before then. Would you like to look upstairs? My sister's not here this time."

"Oh, no hurry, no hurry. That little mama of yours don't scare me, sonny. I'll just take another peek around downstairs, first of all. What's this in here?"

He had crossed the dining room and pushed open the door of the tiny hall leading to Mur's bedroom and bath; Scotty's jaws contracted with resentment but there was nothing to do but follow, saying in as careless a voice as he could summon, "It's just my mother's room, as you can see. I don't think she'd want you in here."

"Yes, well, we just won't tell 'er!" old Suggs whispered with a confidential wink. "I'm not a-gonna touch a thing, just take a little peek. This here her closet? Um-hm . . . built right under the stairs, I see. That's the back of the fireplace, ain't it, that wall there. . . ."

"Yes sir," said Scotty. He managed an anxious glimpse of his watch and instantly forgot what it said.

But old Dorrie's sharp pebble-gray eyes having finished their inspection of Mur's room, moved speculatively to the wall behind her bed, beyond which lay the Nook. He wheeled to start back into the dining room. Scotty shot ahead of him, opened the stairway door and stood holding it suggestively, but old Suggs ambled straight past him, through the living room with his slouching, surprisingly efficient gait, and was in the Nook, eyeing the bookshelves and Mur's battered desk, when Scotty joined him.

"Mr. Suggs, you already saw this room that other time, remember? But upstairs—"

"Oh, I know I saw it, sonny! Been kinda thinking about it, too." To Scotty's despair old Dorrie sat down slowly in the desk chair and folded his knobby hands across his middle as if he meant to think about it some more. He was squinting measuringly at the shelves. "Kind of a liberry, is it?"

"Well, sort of. And my mother uses it as an office." Scotty snatched another glance at his watch. It was 4:37. Perhaps from sheer necessity, he had a flash of inspiration. Casually, he added, "We always thought Great-Gramp used it for that too—did his accounts and stuff here. But we were wrong about that. We found his office the other day."

It took a moment for that to penetrate. Then the glasses flashed his way. "*Found* his office?" said old Dorrie.

"Yeah. At least, we think that's what it was. I mean, it's

actually my bedroom, but couple of days ago our bird got in there, and—"

"Bird?" old Dorrie echoed.

"My sister's parakeet. It tore off some of the wallpaper." Scotty looked as blockheaded as possible, his heart going like a jackhammer. He managed a titter that would have embarrassed him profoundly at any other time. "And wow, were we surprised! There's always been this old joke in our family, see, about Great-Gramp's Money Room, and—"

Old Dorrie was on his feet, the big hands clamped on Scotty's shoulders, the hard gray eyes boring into his. They glared with excitement. *"You found the Money Room?"* he said hoarsely.

"That's what I'm telling you. We—"

"Where?"

"Upstairs, in my—"

Old Dorrie didn't wait. He was taking seven-league strides across the living room and dining room, then up three steps at a time, Scotty puffing exultantly behind him. The hunch was going to work. It was working. And high time—it was now 4:41. "First door on the right," he panted.

Old Dorrie flung open the door, stepped in, and stood stock-still as the full glory of the Money Room burst upon him. Scotty, arriving a second later, stopped in the doorway and watched his face. It was quite a picture—a moving picture, in Living Color; he went quite pale, then flushed like a sunset, like Barney at his best. Slowly a change came over his body— the slight crouch of amazement straightened into a jubilant swagger; he seemed to grow taller before Scotty's eyes, and buoyant, like a balloon. The oversized hands sought their usual shelter of the overalls bib and clasped each other ecstatically underneath it.

"Well!" said old Dorrie in a tone of voice that just missed singing. "Well—well—well! Just lookee there at the nice surprise I've bought me!" He drew a long, expansive breath and flashed a dazzling grin at Scotty. "I knew it was here somewheres. I always knew it! Your great-granpa used to tell me tales about his Money Room—and by golly, here it is. All them shares of things! And now they're *mine*." A knife-sharp glance. "They go with the house, you unnerstand. Anything fastened down belongs to *me*."

Scotty said indifferently, "Yeah, I know. My mother told us."

"She did, eh?" Suggs walked across to pore lovingly over the nearest certificates. But in a moment he turned to squint again at Scotty. "She never took on about it?" Scotty merely shook his head and looked vacant. "Hm. Kinda peculiar. When d'you say all this happened? That bird got in here and all?"

"Friday."

"Friday!" Suggs shook his head. "Must be mistaken, sonny. Your ma and me was together half the afternoon Friday, and she never said a word about it."

"She didn't know it then. I only came up to my room about four-thirty, and she didn't get home till after five." For all Scotty knew, it was after five right now, but he didn't dare look at his watch. The moment had come—almost. . . .

"Good lord a'mighty!" Suggs stared, then suddenly roared with laughter, teetering jubilantly from heel to toe and back. "The same day she sells the place! I'm mighty sorry about that, I really am!" He wiped the tears of merriment from his eyes. "Well, somebody's gotta be the loser if anybody's gonna win. And seems like I'm on a winnin' streak." His voice dropped confidentially. "Tell you a secret, sonny. I gambled I could buy this place for not much more'n the down payment. Fact is, *that* about cleaned me outa cash. But it don't matter. I won my gamble. See these here bank stocks and things? Well, just *one or two* of 'em's enough to take care of the rest of the price. With any luck a-tall!"

Now.

Scotty cleared his throat, tried hard to sound regretful. "Well, I wouldn't count on that, Mr. Suggs. They aren't worth anything. Not any more."

Old Dorrie's laughter was arrested—but only for an instant. He waved the objection away indulgently. "Naw, not all of 'em. 'Course not. Lotta companies went broke in the Big Depression—don't I remember! But your great-granpa, he knew just what he was doin', sonny, believe you me. There'll be a couple or so left that's good as gold—and a couple's plenty. Why, there's dozens of 'em there! And you can't tell me—"

"But I *am* telling you, Mr. Suggs. There's not a one of them on that wall that's any good. We found out."

This time Suggs turned. "You *found out*? How?"

Scotty told him how—in generous detail. It was one of the pleasantest tasks he had ever performed. He named Mr. Berrington, carefully identified the brokerage house of Ames, Berrington, Stokely and Ford as the biggest in the city, and thoughtfully mentioned their address in case Suggs cared to check with them. He reported what he could remember of Mr. Berrington's remarks and dubious headshaking as he scribbled in his notebook. And he wound up by quoting

Mr. Berrington's verdict word for word: " 'There's not a thing on those walls worth more than wallpaper—just as your mother suspected.' My mother never figured they were any good, y'see," Scotty added, getting in a lick for Mur while he was at it. "She's pretty smart about business."

During his recital he had been privileged to watch another Living Color Production. Old Dorrie's ruddy face had gone through crimson to an alarming purple and now was almost gray. He stood motionless, the flashing glasses trained on Scotty like searchlights. Slowly his lips parted; a peculiar-sounding version of his gravelly voice came out: "You . . . she. . . ."

But Scotty had not quite finished. "The only certificate worth anything wasn't even on that wall. We found it ages ago, in a tin box in the attic, with some other old stuff my sister's been playing bank with. Turns out *it's* worth thirty-four thousand dollars." He paused artistically. "But of course that's *ours.*"

Old Dorrie said nothing. Not a word. The glasses stared blindly at Scotty, and the mouth below them worked; whether he was grinding his teeth, or chewing his lip, or furiously biting his own tongue, Scotty couldn't tell. Suddenly he turned and strode from the room, rushed down the stairs, banged his way out of the house—it sounded as if he were bumping into things as he ran. Scotty stumbled after him, a room behind. Just as the screen door clashed like a cymbal against the side of the house, Suggs roared something over his shoulder—it sounded like "—see my lawyer." A moment later the old Pontiac's engine coughed and hiccuped into life, there was an angry spurt of gravel—and he was gone.

It was still three minutes of five. On legs as wobbly as a new kitten's, Scotty tottered to the breakfast nook and collapsed, wondering whether he was entitled now to dance on air or cut his throat. So far, the script had gone the way he'd planned it. But the last act was out of his control.

When Mur came home five minutes later, he was huddled, unseeing, over his math.

CHAPTER XV

Old Suggs didn't come back till seven-thirty. By that time Scotty was exhausted from trying to keep his face impassive, fine-tuning his ears for the sound of tires on gravel, jumping at every unexpected noise and then hastily inventing some action to camouflage the jump.

"Why d'you keep *scratching?*" Lindy asked him irritably during dinner, hitching herself farther away on the breakfast-nook seat.

Scotty mumbled something about mosquitos, reached for the gravy, and scratched no more. Fortunately nobody was interested enough to ask where he found mosquitos in mid-October, and in any case both Mur and Lindy were immersed in their own thoughts—far from happy ones if their expressions were any clue. It was another dinner of which Scotty remembered nothing he ate; by the time they were clearing the table he was sure the last act of his drama had gone awry and it was the moment to cut his throat. When he went upstairs a quarter-hour later he was ready to do it.

Then he heard the car. No mistaking, it was coming up the drive—and it was that Pontiac's engine. He whirled, dashed back downstairs, and seized Mur's elbow.

"Listen. I've got to tell you something."

"*Now*, Scott? Somebody just came up the drive."

"I know! It's old Suggs. What I want to tell you is—he was here earlier. Right after school. Because of me. I phoned and invited him."

"You *what?*" Lindy shrieked. Mur just stared at him.

Scotty swallowed what felt like a large wad of cotton and forged on. "I was—playing a hunch, Mur. Like Great-Gramp. I wanted old Dorrie to see that Money Room. And I showed it to him. And then I—"

"Anybody home?" cried a familiar, jovial, gravelly voice as the screen door banged, and old Dorrie—his usual ruddy, broadly smiling, genial self—slouched into the kitchen, nodding amiable greetings all around. Nobody responded. Fortunately, nobody needed to. Old Dorrie was more than equal to the occasion. "Nice to see you all!" he said enthusiastically. "Fine little family. You got a fine couple kids, Miz Holloway. Pretty little girl—looks a lot the way you usta, don't she? Mighty fine boy, too. Him and me, we're gettin' to be pretty good pals, eh, sonny?"

Scotty, on the receiving end of a happy, confidential wink, felt himself turn into a pillar of salt. Something awful had happened—old Suggs was behaving like a ray of sunshine, which could only mean he'd found some way to swindle them worse than ever.

Mur, standing rigid at Scotty's elbow, murmured something that might have been, "You don't say?"

"Yep, real pals. He done me a real favor this afternoon, that boy of yours," continued old Dorrie. His voice dropped a little; his grin faded. He trained the steel-rimmed glasses earnestly on Mur's face. "He made me realize something I hadn't thought of before. He made me see how much he purely *loves* this place, him and his little sis. It's kinda woke me up, you might say." Suggs looked down at his large, rusty shoes, gave a thoughtful shake to his head, then lifted it bravely. "Well, I come right up to tell you. I just couldn't bring myself to take this farm away from 'em! No sir. Not now."

Beside him, Scotty felt Mur's arm go slack with surprise. His own rock salt began to turn back into flesh and blood and his heart to beat again, rather amateurishly, first fast, then slow. *Why, that old phony*, he thought. Still nobody said anything—except old Dorrie.

"Fact is, I oughta apologize to you, I reckon." His head was cocked, gently rueful. "I kinda rushed you into that deal in the fust place, I'm afraid—mighty fond of this old place myself, y'know. But it don't matter about that. I'm a-gonna let you off the hook."

Mur drew a long, careful breath, and her whole body gradually relaxed. "I see," she said—and aside from the few degrees of frost always reserved for old Suggs, her voice sounded more or less normal. But Scotty heard the tremor of suppressed hilarity in it, and knew she *did* see. She'd suddenly grasped exactly what had happened this afternoon—and that it was working.

Limp with relief, Scotty shot a glance at Lindy, wondering

if she'd caught on too. He needn't have wondered. She was standing stock-still on Mur's other side, her expression that of a joyful spectator at the world's best movie.

Mur was saying, "Well, this is quite a surprise. I thought Dorrit Suggs never backed out of a bargain—even if it was to his advantage."

"I know I said that." Old Dorrie gave her a sheepish look and his most lovable grin. Then he sobered. "But it don't matter. I'm an old man now. Fella my age can't keep on thinking on his own good all the time, considering only hisself. I'm willing to put myself clean in the background, for the sake of them kids." His chin quivered with what Scotty would have sworn was real emotion—and maybe it was; he suspected old Dorrie could convince himself of almost anything, if the occasion demanded.

"All right. If you insist," Mur said. She walked toward the counter beside the breakfast nook, where she'd left her purse.

"Well, I do!" The flashing glasses followed the movement eagerly. "You just tear up them checks I give you Friday, and the deal's off. Just like you wanted."

"Oh, I put those in the bank." Mur rummaged in her purse, produced her checkbook. "But I can write *you* a check for the down payment this minute, and we're quits." She took the cap off her pen, spread the checkbook open on the counter.

"Now, just hold on a second." Suggs's big hand shot up, palm out, then dropped hastily as he substituted an ingratiating smile. "That was *two* checks I give you. One for the down payment, one for earnest money."

"I know," said Mur.

"You'd wanta add in that earnest money, when you write your check."

"No, I wouldn't," Mur informed him.

There was a little silence. Without haste, Mur closed the checkbook on one forefinger, raised her eyes to his face, and waited. Her children gaped at her, exchanged an agonized glance, turned to watch old Dorrie.

His chin was no longer quivering. "Now you listen here, little lady," he said harshly.

"Mr. Suggs," said Mur. "I've had enough of you. Business is business, as you kindly reminded me last night. And everybody knows that when a buyer backs out of a contract, the earnest money's forfeit. We'll play by the rules or I won't play at all and you've got yourself a rundown farm."

The silence this time was breathless, with everybody watching Mur. Lindy suddenly spoke up, her tone knowledgeable.

"You better not push her, Mr. Suggs. She means it. I can tell." Sternly, she added, "There are some things she just can't bring herself to do."

Suggs glared at Lindy, flashed his glasses again to Mur, and turned his back. "Have it your way!" he growled.

That was the end of it, really. Scotty, now constructed entirely of taut rubber and helium, strained to keep his feet anchored to the floor and his bubbling, jubilant mirth from exploding all over the kitchen, while Mur wrote her check, tore it out and waved it dry, and handed it to Suggs. He took it glumly, examined it and lifted a face that had become that of a sad and broken man.

"I never thought I'd be treated so shameful by the granddaughter of my old, true friend," he quavered. "No sir, I'd never of believed it, not if I'd been told by ever'body in town. . . ."

There was more, but it died away as Mur ushered him firmly out. Scotty and Lindy seized each other's arms and performed a silent, wild fandango, which ended only when Mur reappeared in the doorway. Scotty looked toward her and saw her eyes bright with laughter, her face alive again—just as Barney's dad's had been on *his* lucky day—and knew that this was what he'd been longing for and playing hunches for, and that it was well worth everything.

"You can go ahead and cheer," Mur said. "He's gone."

A war whoop went up, led deafeningly by Lindy and joined by Gretel, who woke up in her basket beside the stove and began to bark indignantly. Mur, laughing a bit hysterically, walked straight to Scotty and hugged him hard. "Oh, Scotty, how did you *do* it? Whatever gave you the notion? Oh, you great kid! Tell us what happened!"

"Yeah! How'd you break it to him? What'd he say?" Lindy demanded.

So Scotty told them, omitting none of old Sugg's Technicolor movie effects or his own frantic clock-watching, and they marveled at him and asked gloating questions, and it was all supremely satisfactory. Afterwards Mur took a long ecstatic breath, clasped her hands in front of her, and looked all around the kitchen with a gleam in her eye.

"I'm going to paint this whole room white, with yellow trim," she said. "And then I'm going to get that flagstone-pattern linoleum for the floor, and an up-to-date stove. And after that I'm going to panel the Nook and get new living room curtains and repaper my bedroom—yours too, Lindy—and fix all the dry rot and get the house painted and a new screen door. . . ."

As Scotty and Lindy stared around them, dazzled, trying to visualize all this coming grandeur, Mur took an arm of each and pushed them gently to the breakfast nook. Then she sat down across from them.

"And you know what else I want to do with that thirty-four thousand—and old Dorrie's earnest money? That is, if it's okay with you vice-presidents." Again, she clasped her hands, this time on the table where they clung to each other tightly. "I want to go halves with Walt Thatcher on the picking machine. He still needs five thousand to buy it outright from Henry, and I want to supply that—if he'll let me—and we can go into business together. It would mean extra income right now, while I'm settling in at the office—and every harvest season from now on too. Well—what do you say?"

"Wow!" exclaimed Scotty, picturing Barney's face when he heard. "So he won't even need to get the loan?"

"Not if he agrees to let me in as partner."

"Well, he will, won't he?" Lindy cried. "Mur, phone right now and ask him!"

"I will!" Mur's Lindy-grin appeared as she bumped the table getting up. Then she stopped. "Oh. No, I won't. The Thatchers don't have a phone. Scotty? Run over there and get Walt, would you? See if he'll come talk to me about it—we could settle the whole thing now, tonight."

Scotty ran, bounding out of the house and across the dusky back yard, heading for the creek and the short cut Barney had shown him. He felt as if he could fly all the way. *Everything* was okay now, the house was theirs, the orchard was theirs, the Old Scott Place was going to be the Holloway Place—forever, he hoped, because he'd never loved any place as well. At least—of course he'd loved Cherry Street just as well, but—

Struggling with a sudden feeling of disloyalty, Scotty thought: *But that was then—and this is now,* and felt the guilt clearing from his mind as he finally understood that puzzling bit from Great-Gramp's journal. Of course he'd loved Cherry Street and having Dad to hold up the world, and that whole life. But he'd *had* those good years—and still had them, in his memory, as part of him, just as Great-Gramp had said. Nobody and nothing could ever take them away.

Now he had *this*—he flung his arms wide in an all-encompassing gesture—all this, plus Great-Gramp's hovering ghost to ask for advice whenever he needed it. And maybe he was beginning—just barely—to learn to hold up the world for himself.

He no longer wanted to go back to anything. He wanted to go straight ahead.